Reader reviews of ~~Magic Flag~~ Mystery

★★★★★ Readers ⸻ ⸻ Detective stories, a mod⸻ ⸻ ,h it is a story aimed for kid⸻ ⸻ nd thrills and spills to captivate any adult ⸻

★★★★★ Finished reading The Magic Flag Mystery (I'm a big wean at heart). Brilliant story, fantastic Detective Team, so capturing from start to finish, cheering them on at times and my heart in my mouth other times, I'll let you find out for yourselves when you read it.

★★★★★ What a wonderful story. Read in one sitting. Little tear in the eye at the end with a big smile.

★★★★★ I really loved this story! It's a bit like an Enid Blyton adventure set on the wonderful island of Skye. I love the connection between the characters whether human, dog or even bird! It's swift moving and twists and turns as tension builds. An excellent read.

★★★★★ The scenery and atmosphere of Skye are captured perfectly. Blaze is a typical Border Collie - very intelligent and eager to be active. The story is well-paced, with enough excitement and adventure to keep children of all ages enthralled.

★★★★★ I absolutely loved reading this book. I am also very honoured and humble to have met Blaze and Laoch so it really brought the book to life for me.

Reader reviews of *The Magic Flag Mystery*

★★★★★ A story for all ages. I recommend this book for people who love a mystery, who want to be transported to the Isle of Skye, who enjoy a wee laugh at the antics of Laoch and for those that have a psychic connection with their dog (but don't want to admit it).

★★★★★ A terrific book for every age, young and old. Blaze and his Detective Team are terrific, the pace keeps you turning the page and the descriptive writing paints vivid pictures in your mind as you swim in the cave with Blaze or chase the rabbits with Laoch.

★★★★★ This is a fantastic story ideal for children who love animals, adventure and legends. There is just the right balance of adventure with a slight hint of danger, enough to excite but not so much that would frighten active young minds. Children will love it, I did and I'm just a big wean at heart.

★★★★★ Good grief, I'm an adult & I found this book brilliant, heartstopping moments, wary anticipation. This is a well paced book, about the Blaze detective team, it's a great scamper across Skye. I suppose I'll have to let my daughter read it now.

★★★★★ A terrific book for every age, young and old. Read and enjoy.

Blaze Dog Detective

In

The Magic Flag Mystery

by

Lin Anderson & Donald McKay

First published in Scotland in 2020
by Dunedin Media
Reprinted September 2020

ISBN 978-1-8380380-0-7

http://www.dunedinmedia.co.uk

The Magic Flag Mystery

Chapter One

A Surprise Visitor

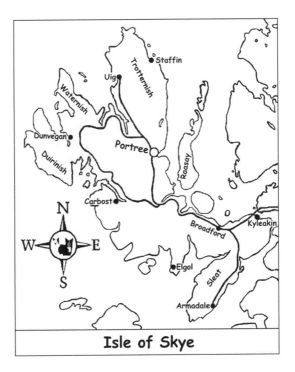

Isle of Skye

Hi. I'm Blaze, dog detective. I live on the Isle of Skye with my wee brother Laoch, who's also a Border Collie, and my human Dad. I'm mostly black and shaggy with brown eyes, while Laoch (pronounced Loo-och) is mostly white, with one blue eye and one brown.

Skye is a big island off the west coast of Scotland. The

island is famous for lots of things, including mountains and great beaches. We also have three castles.

How did I become a dog detective, you might ask? Well, the idea probably began when I helped the Skye and Lochaber Police to find a missing person in the mountains using my excellent scenting skills.

Dad can tell by smell when he's put sugar in his tea. Me, I could scent that spoonful of sugar in an Olympic size swimming pool. That's how good my nose is.

I'm scenting at the moment, and running, and panting because I am chasing something, but it's not a robber. Not this time. I'm chasing a rabbit, which I'm sorry to say, is faster than me, and definitely better at hiding.

I now realise that this particular rabbit, a big grey one with a floppy ear has won. Again. So I stop running and take a seat.

From the top of the hill behind our home I can see the road to the Fairy Glen, another of Skye's famous landmarks. It also leads to one of the castles I mentioned earlier. Dunvegan, home of the Fairy Flag, an ancient relic of the Clan MacLeod, as precious to them as Scotland's Crown Jewels are to the people of Scotland.

From here I can also watch the road that comes up from Portree and eventually I spot what I'm looking for.

Hurrah!

I take off, faster on the way down, than on the way up. I'm almost back at our cottage, Taigh na Collie (the house of the Collies) when I hear the startling bark of my wee brother Laoch. So he's spotted who's coming too.

The roar of the motorbike approaching has Laoch jumping and twirling in the air with excitement. I'm excited too, but I just give one of my happy barks.

As the red motorbike roars through the gate, I realise it looks different and there's more than just Granny Beaton on it.

Granny B's no ordinary granny, Dad says. She used to travel about Scotland in a horse drawn caravan. Now she lives on a croft above Portree and travels about Skye on her red motorbike. She also has a crystal ball!

Tonight, my pal Rory is riding pillion on the famous bike, and Granny's also attached her wee sidecar and…wait a minute… there's someone in it.

It's a girl I've never seen before.

Parked up now, Granny gives one of her high whistles that no one but Laoch and I can hear. This makes Laoch stop his leaping about and he immediately sits down as still as a statue. Me, I also wait as instructed by that whistle, while Granny takes off her black helmet with the red flame and opens the door of the sidecar to let the girl out.

3

She's small, maybe ten years in human age, with long wild curly brown hair. She looks a little hesitant as though she's just entered a classroom full of school bullies.

I wag my tail and give her one of my best smiles as if to say, any friend of Granny Beaton's a friend of mine.

'This is Rosa,' Granny says. 'My granddaughter. She's come from Glasgow to live with me on Skye.' Granny and Dad exchange looks as though he knows something about all of this already. I wanted to ask why she'd come to live on Skye and where her parents were.

At this point, Rosa's eyes met mine, and the funny thing is, I could see exactly what she was thinking. This gave me quite a shock, I can tell you. Dad and I have what he calls a *rapport*, which I think means he gives me orders and I obey. Laoch not so much, but he's still young and learning. I can often tell what Dad's thinking, but it doesn't work both ways.

Not like what was happening right now.

I could see Rosa in the back seat of a car. There was a terrible screech of tyres, a crashing sound and then her world flipped over.

Rosa took her sad eyes from mine and the moment ended. I gave a little whine and went up to her and nuzzled her hand and I seemed to hear her say 'thank you' although it wasn't out loud.

4

'Welcome to Taigh na Collie, Rosa,' Dad said, and then he and Granny were talking about lighting the outside fire and cooking some burgers, plus sausages for the boys (that's me and Laoch). Laoch recognising the word sausages went back to his air twirls.

As Dad and Granny B set about their preparations, Rory asked Rosa if she wanted to take a look around.

I like Rory. He's tall and gangly, with wild hair and a serious face, except when he grins. Dad says he's a loner, who likes animals more than humans. His dad's a fisherman who's at sea a lot. Rory has a canoe and I go out with him in it sometimes. Laoch's not allowed to go with us until he learns to swim. My wee brother hasn't got past the paddling stage yet.

Rosa gives a little nod and I realise I haven't heard her speak yet. I try to imagine her spoken voice. What will it be like?

'Coming?' Rory says to me.

Of course I am. Laoch on the other hand has smelt the meat brought out to cook on the fire which is already crackling. For Laoch food always comes first.

I go in front, knowing where Rory will take this little girl with the sad thoughts. He'll take her to the wooden fort on top of the hill. He'll help her climb up to the top.

Rory will show her the island that's going to be her

new home, but he won't ask her why she had to come here. Nor where her parents are.

Me? I think I know the answer to that already.

The smell of food greets us on our return.

'Come on guys,' Dad says. 'Get stuck in.'

We all sat round the fire after we'd scoffed all the food. Dad played his guitar for a bit, singing some Skye songs to make Rosa feel at home. Laoch joined in, which wasn't good. His howl is as startling as his bark.

Granny Beaton and Dad talked a bit in low voices after that, while Rosa stared into the flames, her cheeks rosy with the heat. It was about school. I've been into the local school a couple of times to demonstrate my excellent scenting skills. The children hide something in the classroom and I have to find it!

I didn't know what they were saying exactly, but I could tell by their expressions that it wasn't good. When I looked over at Rosa, she met my gaze again and then I knew. The way she'd looked when she first stepped out of the sidecar, was the way she'd felt when taken to the school.

In her thoughts she was in the playground, and a boy was shouting at her. Calling her a words I didn't know. *Tinker. Gypsy.* What did that mean?

'Okay,' Granny B was saying, 'time to go home.' She

turned to Rosa. 'Last day of school tomorrow, and Blaze is coming in to do some of his tricks.'

Tricks! I might have taken offence at that, but didn't. They might think of them as tricks, but it was really just good detective work.

Dad said he would run Rory home.

'See you tomorrow,' Rory said to Rosa as she climbed in the sidecar.

I thought her face lifted a little at that. At least she would have one more friendly face other than myself at her new school tomorrow.

'That's one sad little girl,' Dad said as he waved them off. 'You'll need to watch out for her, Rory.'

I barked then, because I had already decided that was going to be my job too.

Chapter Two

Detective Tricks!

Looking out at my young audience, I decided that being in school on the last day of term was more fun than chasing that big grey floppy-eared rabbit.

Rory was there, sitting up the back with the older pupils. Rosa was in the middle. I'd spotted her as soon as Dad brought me in. Surrounded by other children, she still looked lost and alone and when I met her eye, I knew she was.

I immediately barked my hello and went up to her to show the others that we were friends. That brought a smile from Rosa, and a look of interest from the other pupils, especially the boy I'd seen in her thoughts who'd called Rosa names.

After that I started my 'tricks'.

The first was to find the head teacher, Mr Stewart. That was too easy, so I took my time nosing among the children causing much laughter before I revealed his presence in the store cupboard to lots of cheering.

The second was to find the owner of a schoolbag. I was given the bag to sniff and then off I went running this way and that, while the children laughed and shouted 'hot' and 'cold' to help me. I didn't need any help of course. I knew whose bag it was.

Dan, I realised, was a little afraid of me. So I didn't bark at him, but went quietly up and dropped the bag at his feet to a big cheer from my audience.

My task complete, I was given my treat by Mr Stewart and then the children were allowed to come and pat me. I was pleased to see Rory speaking to a now smiling Rosa. It looked like my detective team was about to have a new member.

I am of course the best at scenting. Laoch has much to learn, but he's getting there. Dad says the fact that he has one blue eye and one brown means he can look at heaven and earth at the same time. I don't know about that, but my wee brother certainly has a keen eye.

Rory knows Skye better than anyone, plus Dad and Granny B trust him, which means he gets to be in charge of us. If you're solving mysteries you don't want adults hanging about all the time.

Adding Rosa to our gang, especially since we could 'talk' to one another was a great idea.

Rosa looked directly at me and I knew exactly what she was thinking. She'd love to join Team Blaze.

As Mr Stewart started to wish everyone a happy holiday, a figure appeared at the door of the classroom. It was Police Constable Munro from the Portree Police Station, who I've helped with searches a few times. He's normally a cheery policeman, but today he looked serious. The head teacher and PC Munro went into a huddle, then Mr Stewart called us all to be quiet.

It seemed there was bad news coming.

'I know you were all looking forward to the annual summer party at Dunvegan Castle tomorrow, children. I'm sorry to say that it has had to be cancelled.'

A babble of disappointment filled the room.

'What's happened?' Dad said, looking worried.

It was PC Munro who answered. 'There's been a break in at the castle. The Fairy Flag has been stolen.'

Now the babble turned to dismay. Every child in that room had been brought up on the story of the Fairy Flag gifted to the Clan MacLeod to keep them safe in battle. Missing the summer castle party was one thing, but losing the flag was much worse.

PC Munro tried to reassure them. 'We have a full team on this, kids. We will find the people who stole the flag. That's why I'm here. To ask Blaze to join us in the search.'

There were a few claps at that which cheered everyone up, including me.

As Mr Stewart dismissed the children, PC Munro came

up to us.

'How'd they get into the tower room?' Dad asked.

'We have no idea. The big door was still locked and, as you know, there's no way in or out of the tower except by that door. It's a mystery, plus a disaster for the open day with the kids and the rest of the summer tourist season. Most tourists who visit Skye come to see the Fairy Flag.'

PC Munro was right. For Skye having the Fairy Flag stolen was as terrible as the Crown Jewels being taken from Edinburgh Castle.

Rosa and Rory had come over to join us and Rosa was listening intently to everything PC Munro was saying.

'The Clan Chief asked if you could bring Blaze over to see if he can pick up a scent of how the burglars got in there.'

At the mention of my name I gave a low bark. Of course I wanted to go.

'Sounds like Blaze is already on the job,' Dad said with a smile.

Heading out to the jeep, we found Laoch with the janitor, getting petted by the departing pupils.

'How did he do?' Dad said.

'He watched through the window for a bit, then chased rabbits in the woods.'

'Catch anything?' Dad said already knowing the

answer.

'Nope. But that might be because he warns them very loudly that he's coming.'

Dad thanked the janitor for keeping an eye on my wee brother and we all climbed in the truck.

Rosa sat between me and Laoch in the back and we had a conversation. Not out loud, of course. Now that she seemed a little less sad, I found it was even easier to read her thoughts. I also knew she was practising reading mine.

As we headed for the castle, Rosa told us what she knew about the Fairy Flag.

'Granny Beaton says Clan MacLeod go all the way back to the Vikings and King Harald Hardrada of Norway,' Rosa said. 'Harald brought a magic flag with him, which became the Fairy Flag of the MacLeods. Legend says if the MacLeods were in danger on the battlefield, the flag unfurled makes them invincible.'

'Well we're in a battle now,' Rory said. 'The battle to get it back.'

Rosa's eyes met mine. Gone was the sadness and the fear. Replaced by determination.

For a moment I saw the fragile flag in its glass case in her thoughts. Then it was whole again, unfurled and waving in the breeze. And guess who was waving it?

Our Rosa.

Chapter Three

The Castle

The Chief of Clan MacLeod was waiting at the castle entrance for us.

'Thank you for coming,' he said. 'I'd like Blaze to take a look in the tower room, hopefully pick up a scent.'

'Can I go with Blaze?' Rosa said quietly. We understand one other.' She looked at me and I barked in agreement.

'Rosa has a special way with animals, ' Dad explained. 'Especially with Blaze.'

Laoch, sensing something was up, bounced about like the donkey from Shrek crying, 'Pick me. Pick me'.

Thankfully Dad was having none of that. 'Stay, Laoch.'

Asking Laoch to 'stay' is a bit like asking a burn to stop flowing, and with as little chance of success. Laoch does 'stay' for a bit, to make it look like he's obeying orders, but once eyes are off him, he thinks that time's up, and goes wherever he likes.

As the Clan Chief beckoned Rosa and I to follow him, I gave Laoch a look, which in doggy terms said, 'Examine the area. We'll talk later.'

Laoch's grin indicated he'd got the message. The likelihood was that he would scurry here and there and achieve nothing, especially if he spotted a rabbit, but he had to be given a job, if he was to be part of Team Blaze.

As for Rory, I sent him off to ask his Uncle Calum, who ran the seal trips from the castle, if the castle staff had any clues about the robbery.

As Rosa and I walked with Dad and the Clan Chief up the drive, a cloud of crows rose from the battlements, swirling and cawing angrily above us.

'The birds have been behaving like this ever since we discovered the robbery,' the Clan Chief said looking up at the darkened sky. 'It's as if they know that something's wrong.'

As we climbed the wide staircase, I could sense Rosa's wonder at being in the castle for the first time, and her fear at what we would find there.

When we entered the tower room and saw the shattered glass case, Rosa gasped. I felt the same. The Fairy Flag

14

was the heart of the castle, and the heart had gone. It was as though she could hear all those MacLeods through the ages weeping.

And Rosa wept silently with them, tears running down her cheeks. As for me, I can't cry. Not that way, but I could still show my sadness. I whined a little and shoved my cold nose into Rosa's hand.

She turned then and wiping away her tears, silently reminded me why we were there.

Of course, I hadn't forgotten. I may not have looked like it, but that nose of mine was doing its job. So while my cold nozzle was nudging Rosa in sympathy, my scenting powers were working the room, and coming up with results.

Sensing Rosa's wish that I should do a full investigation, I left her standing just inside the door and went about my business. And I was thorough. By the time I had finished I was pretty sure I would recognise the scent of everyone who had been in that room recently.

But that wasn't all I'd caught in my examination.

When I returned to Rosa, she crouched down to my level and gave me one of her penetrating stares. It was like having every thought in your head hoovered up.

'There's been another dog in here too, hasn't there?' Rosa said silently.

I barked, because Rosa was right.

Chapter Four

The Tower Room

When we'd first entered the Fairy Tower, we'd been totally focussed on our search for clues. Now having satisfied ourselves on that, Rosa and I silently agreed to admire the room where the famous flag should have been.

The oak wood panels that lined the walls smelt as fresh to my nose as the day the trees had been cut down. Rosa ran her hand gently over them marvelling at the smoothness.

Then came the weapons, long claymores (big heavy swords) and giant battle axes. Studded targes (shields) completed the picture. When she moved to the paintings, Rosa read out the names of all the former chiefs of Clan MacLeod and I liked the sound of them rolling off her tongue.

When she came to the final painting, it was as though this was the one Rosa had wanted to study all along.

The painting was of a battlefield, with a man on a horse leading the charge, but behind him I now saw what looked like an older Rosa, holding the Fairy Flag in one hand and a sword in the other. It was the image I'd seen in her thoughts earlier.

Had an ancestor of Rosa's been a warrior maiden who'd carried the Fairy Flag into battle?

'Are you two finished up in here yet?' The Clan Chief's voice suddenly broke the spell the painting had conjured up.

Rosa said that we were and told the him about the dog I'd scented in the room.

'That's strange,' he said. 'Dogs aren't permitted in the castle, only the grounds.'

'We're certain a dog has been in here,' Rosa said, and I added an accompanying bark as confirmation.

'If the dog was with the robbers, how did they all get in?' the Clan Chief said.

That was a question we couldn't answer… yet.

As we exited the castle, I realised something else was troubling Rosa. Something I couldn't 'see' at first. Moments later, I suddenly knew what that worry was.

We didn't interrupt Dad and the Clan Chief as they discussed our findings. We weren't even sure if there was time for that. We just ran like the wind towards the image that I'd seen in Rosa's head, me taking the lead, but only because I had four legs.

Rosa was a fast runner, and there wasn't any doubt in my mind that she knew exactly where we were going.

I got to the jetty by the loch seconds before Rosa did to

find the water completely calm and clear right to the bottom, and yet I'd definitely seen Laoch thrashing about in there in Rosa's thoughts.

Where was my wee brother? Had he already drowned and been washed out to sea?

I barked in the hope that his own startling bark would answer in return, but it didn't. I have never missed hearing Laoch's bark more than I did at that moment.

Just then Rosa caught up with me, looking wildly round just the way I had done. Like me she began searching the water, kneeling down better to see to the bottom.

'He's not there,' I heard her say. 'Laoch's not there. But I saw him sink. I imagined him thrashing about down there as though he was drowning.'

'I tried to teach him to swim,' I told her silently. 'I tried, but he wouldn't listen. He just liked paddling and chasing crabs along the shore, and scaring the seagulls that dared to land near us.'

Rosa stood up, the expression on her face suddenly changing from despair to hope. It was as though she had caught something on the wind. I immediately tested the air myself. Surely if Laoch was anywhere nearby, my legendary scenting powers would find him, even if he was under the water?

Then I heard her whistle just like Granny B's, high and clear to me, but inaudible to any of the people nearby.

It was his startling bark that reached us first, although it did sound a little hoarse, before Laoch arrived at full speed from the direction of the castle cafe. He was bounding along the path towards us, looking mightily pleased with himself.

When he got closer I noticed a long piece of seaweed trailing from his hair, and his coat did look very wet. Maybe we had been right when we'd imagined him in the water?

If we were, and it certainly looked like it, he'd got out successfully. Thank goodness. Not only that, he'd managed a trip to the cafe and had definitely begged a sausage roll from there. The clue to this being the pastry crumbs caught in his wet beard.

The jumping about ceased as Rosa knelt down and 'gave Laoch the eye', like she does with me. As she interrogated him, I listened in.

It seems Laoch had decided that if someone wanted to creep into the grounds of Castle Dunvegan at night unseen, they would come by boat.

Wow, I was quite impressed with my wee brother's thinking.

It seems Laoch had headed for the shore, then spent

time chasing some crabs. (typical Laoch!) until his blue eye caught sight of something glinting in the water next to the jetty.

He headed along the jetty to take a closer look and that's when it all went wrong. The end of the jetty was green and slippery and my poor wee brother had slipped and slithered and fallen in!

Down he'd gone, both eyes open. That's when he spotted the shiny object that had caught his attention in the first place.

When Laoch revealed that he'd suddenly discovered he could swim, thanks to remembering my instructions, Rosa burst out laughing.

Dogs don't laugh of course, but we can do a mighty big smile and a bit of joyful panting, which I did.

Kneeling down, Rosa peered into the water. 'There it is,' she said, and taking off her sandals, she dropped in.

I panicked a little at this but then remembered since I was an excellent swimmer, I could pull her to shore with my teeth if anything went wrong.

Rosa began searching among the stones and seaweed on the bottom and minutes later, she shouted, 'Got it!' her voice triumphant.

Laoch had gone back to skipping about on the jetty again, his paws slithering on the wet and slippery

21

seaweed.

Look at the name. Look at the name, he was telling us.

I heard the name emerge from Rosa's mouth and it sounded fierce, but not as fierce as the image of a dog she had conjured up in her brain. She offered the name tag to me, placing it on the jetty for me to sniff.

And I did just that. Didn't I tell you I could smell a spoonful of sugar in an Olympic sized swimming pool? Well that name tag might have been in the water, but there was no doubt in my nose that it had been worn by the same dog that had been in the Fairy Tower room.

And that dog, according to the name tag was called FANG!

Chapter Five

The Crystal Ball

It was Rosa who decided how much to tell Dad about Laoch's escapades on the jetty. He learned about Laoch falling in and discovering he could swim, and the suspicion that the thieves may have arrived by boat. What she didn't mention was the name tag.

I wondered why, but I knew Rosa would have her reasons.

'The boat is definitely a possibility,' Dad said. 'We'll mention that to PC Munro.' Then he turned to Laoch. 'So you're a swimmer now?' Dad said, obviously delighted by the news.

I wasn't sure that Laoch knew what Dad meant. He grinned anyway, but I suspected the happy smile was more about discovering the dog tag, and less to do with his new found swimming skills.

'Don't worry, I'm sure the Skye and Lochaber Police will find the Fairy Flag,' Dad told us as we made for the truck.

With our help, I heard Rosa silently say.

The story of the missing flag had travelled round Skye like wildfire. When we reached home, our neighbour

Matt, who runs A.C.E Target Sports nearby, immediately appeared to ask us about the robbery. Even the group of visitors who'd been learning archery with him crowded round to hear the tale.

As Dad described what had happened, Rosa told Laoch and me that she wanted us to talk alone, so I led her to a little secluded spot beside the burn.

I waited, trying to see what was on Rosa's mind. It wasn't easy. There were a lot of swirling thoughts in there, as she sat contemplating the little pool of water I particularly liked to paddle in.

When Rosa didn't say anything, Laoch grew restless, and eventually, drawn no doubt by the scent of a rabbit, darted off.

When I barked at him to come back, Rosa laid a hand on my head to stop me.

'It's okay,' she seemed to say. 'Let Laoch have fun. We don't need him at the moment.'

I wondered what or who we were waiting for, because Rosa didn't say, neither was there anything obvious swirling round in her thoughts. Or at least nothing I recognised. Occasionally the image of that painting would appear for a moment, followed by the oak panel next to it in the Fairy Flag room.

Rosa did seem to be very interested in that panel.

I was brought back out of my reverie by a noise I immediately recognised.

Now the image in Rosa's thoughts was quite clear and consisted of a picture that matched the welcome sound of an approaching motorbike.

'Granny Beaton's here,' Rosa announced, and springing up, hurried towards the car park, with me taking the lead.

Granny swept through the open gate and skilfully parking her bike and sidecar, came to greet us. Crouching down, she stared into my eyes. It was quite strange to have a woman in a helmet give you 'the eye', but I managed.

'So, Rosa,' she said, standing up, 'I see from Blaze you have a lead on the thief who stole the Fairy Flag?'

How did she get all of that from looking at me, I wondered.

As though she'd heard my thoughts, Granny said, 'I think it's time for the crystal ball.'

My eyes grew big as Granny Beaton opened one of her saddle bags and proceeded to rummage around inside it.

Of course I'd heard about the crystal ball. I'd even seen it once. But was I actually going to see it in action?

Rosa looked as wide-eyed as me. 'I didn't think you would have it with you Granny.'

'I was doing a little charitable fortune telling in Portree.'

Granny, finding what she was searching for, pulled it out with a, 'Here it is!'

Being summer and a pleasant day, the sun found and touched the crystal ball as it emerged. It was like being struck by a star. I blinked a few times to dispel the rainbow that blinded my eyes, and gave a soft growl of appreciation.

'Right,' said Granny. 'Let's find a good place.'

Granny immediately led us up further up the side of the burn past where we had been sitting before, until we reached a little clearing among the birch trees, in the middle of which stood an old tree trunk covered with moss.

'Just the spot,' Granny B said.

On the way there, Rosa had, I think, told Granny the full story of what had happened that morning including the almost drowning episode.

Granny had laughed aloud at this.

'Where is Laoch?' I heard her say.

Rosa shook her head, indicating she didn't know.

So Granny did the whistle she had taught Rosa. I heard it too, and knew if I hadn't already been here, I would definitely be on my way now.

Laoch obviously heard it too, because it wasn't long before we heard the crackling of undergrowth and the thud of paws. My wee brother, never one to enter a room quietly, burst into the clearing and made straight for Granny Beaton, then proceeded to do his springing into the air bit, even managing a turn or two as he did so.

There was another whistle and suddenly all was calm and Laoch sat down and awaited whatever Granny had called him for.

Granny Beaton now turned her attention to the tree trunk where the crystal ball sat. As she did so, a shaft of sunlight broke through the surrounding birch trees and fastened on the crystal globe, dazzling my eyes for a moment.

I blinked but didn't look away and soon I saw a mist fill the crystal ball, a bit like the mist I saw in Rosa's thoughts before they became a picture.

Rosa had drawn closer to the crystal ball and was staring intently at it, just like me. I had a sudden recall of the scent of oak wood in the Fairy Flag room, quite distinct from the smell of the birch trees that surrounded us.

The mist cleared and there was the painting Rosa had so admired...and...there we both were in the crystal ball standing next to the painting.

27

'The girl in the painting,' Granny said. 'She looks a bit like you, Rosa.'

I heard Granny's voice, but it sounded far away. I was here and there at the same time. Laoch seeing us in the crystal ball, gave a little whine as though he was sad that he'd been left out.

Now Rosa was stroking the wood, just as she had done in the room earlier, drawing closer and closer to the big painting as she did so.

There was a click, as clear to my ears as one of Rosa's whistles... and the panel moved.

All four of us watched in amazement as the panel swung open and we were looking into a long dark tunnel from which, to my nose certainly, came a strong smell of the sea.

'That's how they got into the Fairy Flag room,' Rosa said.

Chapter Six

The Secret Passage

The mist came swirling back into the crystal ball and the image disappeared.

'Well,' Granny said in obvious amazement. 'I never knew there was a secret passage.' She looked quite put out by that.

'You told me about the Sea Gate, Granny,' Rosa reminded her, 'how that was the only entrance through the wall that surrounds the castle.'

'That wasn't the Sea Gate we saw, although,' Granny Beaton glanced at me, 'Blaze here could smell the sea.'

I made a sound to indicate she was right about that.

'The Sea Gate is open to the public,' Granny went on. 'There are photographs of it on the internet and it definitely doesn't run between Dunvegan Loch and the Fairy Tower.' She looked to Rosa, as though expecting her to have something else to say.

Rosa had on her faraway look she wears sometimes. The look Granny calls her second sight. If someone has the second sight it means they can sometimes see into the future.

Just then excited shouts came from the woods. Laoch,

deciding he'd reached his attention span, checked Granny for permission, then darted back into the trees.

From a distance we could hear the current Airsoft battle being played out at the wooden fort on the hilltop. One half of Matt's customers had obviously reached there and were holding the other half at bay.

For a moment it reminded me of the painting of another battle long ago.

'We have to go back,' Rosa said. 'And check to see if the crystal ball is telling the truth.'

I thought Granny Beaton might take umbrage at the suggestion that her crystal ball might lie, but she didn't.

'Exactly,' she said. 'The ball sometimes shows us only what we wish to see.'

I felt a bit disappointed about that. I had assumed the opposite, that the crystal ball told you the truth about the future, or about things you needed to know.

Rosa was talking to Granny Beaton, explaining what she thought we should do, and I was picking up the message loud and clear. She wanted us to return to the castle with Granny and we would go there by motorbike. I saw that image in her head, but it was only Rosa and Granny Beaton on the motorbike.

Where was Blaze Dog Detective? Surely they wouldn't leave me behind?

Then I saw myself in Rosa's thoughts and I was in the sidecar just like Rosa had been last night.

Hurrah! Rosa was suggesting to Granny that I went with them in the sidecar.

After this discussion we went in search of Dad who had in fact been looking for us.

Granny Beaton explained that we wanted to go back to the castle, although she didn't explain why. She just said that we were following up on a possible clue.

He thought for a moment and I knew what he was going to say.

'Better that Laoch stays with me since he's not allowed inside the castle.'

I was a little relieved about that. I had no idea what it would be like to travel in a sidecar and kept imagining Laoch jumping about in it in his usual fashion. It was a scary thought.

Knowing I liked an open window in our truck, Granny left the top of the sidecar down and got me to jump inside. Luckily Laoch hadn't appeared back yet, so I wasn't worried that he might jump in too.

Then we were off.

Granny B honked her horn to say goodbye, then the wind was ruffling my coat and freezing my nose as the scents rushed past.

31

I'd travelled this single track road from our house to Dunvegan many times before, but always in the truck. This time I felt as though I was running over the moorland, my hair blowing back in the wind. I decided at that moment that I liked going by motorbike and sidecar better than any other method of travel.

Granny was a bit of a speedster, or maybe it was because I was much closer to the ground than in the truck. Anyway, I tried not to think about how fast we were going, but just looked out at places that seemed familiar, yet so different and more exciting from the open sidecar.

We passed a few cars on the way and they all waved at us. I couldn't wave back but I wore my big panting smile instead and tried to look like a detective out on the job.

Dad must have phoned ahead to the Clan Chief to warn him of our return visit, because he was waiting for us in the same place as before.

I immediately jumped out of the sidecar and went to greet him. The Chief and I have known each other since I was a pup and like Dad, he has a special way with animals and has a few dogs of his own.

He ruffled my ears and murmured something welcoming. When Rosa and Granny had taken of their helmets and stowed them in the sidecar, they joined us.

Granny and he had a conversation, after which they led

32

the way across the bridge to the big entrance. Rosa placed her hand on my head as we walked and through her touch I knew what she was intent on doing.

I could tell by the Chief's manner, that he was very worried about the Fairy Flag. Our arrival with perhaps a clue as to what might have happened, was giving him some cause for hope. I could only hope myself that the image we'd seen in the crystal ball was not a false one.

As we climbed the stairs towards the Fairy Tower, the castle, empty of visitors appeared very forlorn. The closer we got to the Fairy room, the sadder the castle became.

Looking up at Rosa, I saw that she felt the same, but although sad, she was also determined. Once inside, Granny suggested she and the Chief leave us alone, because Rosa would need all her concentration.

When the door shut behind them, we stood for a moment, before Rosa, touching my head to follow, walked towards the painting of the battle. I thought she looked so small in front of the huge portrait, yet there was the other older Rosa tall and strong up there with the Fairy Flag unfurled.

After a few moments, Rosa stepped forward and began to stroke the oak panel on the left hand side of the painting. At that moment, something happened to my hair, for I felt it spring up in the way it did when Dad gave me a good brush.

I could hear Rosa's heart as clearly as a drumbeat and to my eye there was a glow about her, just like the girl in the painting.

When I heard the click it startled me, although I'd really wanted it to happen. As the door sprang inwards, I looked into a dark passageway. Then came the smell of the sea to wrinkle my nose.

That wasn't the only scent I was picking up. A dog had been in this passage recently and I knew for certain who that dog was.

Fang!

Without checking with Rosa, I immediately sprang through the opening.

Seconds later there was a loud click, the panel shut with a snap and I was plunged into darkness.

Chapter Seven

Trapped

Why had the secret door suddenly closed before Rosa could follow me into the tunnel?

I gave a sharp bark and awaited a response, which didn't come. No sound of Rosa on the other side of the secret door and despite my efforts, no pictures of her thoughts inside my head either.

I nosed at the panel hoping my touch might cause it to spring open again. It didn't.

I was alone in the darkness of the secret passage and without Rosa. What should I do?

Instinct told me to carry on and find out where the tunnel went, for surely this was how the thieves with Fang must have entered the tower room?

It was at that point Rosa's thoughts drifted into my head. 'Go,' she seemed to be saying. 'Find the tunnel entrance, Blaze. Go!'

I set off, not running but taking my time, picking up two human scents on the way, both of which I'd encountered recently and definitely in the tower room.

Which meant they could belong to the robbers!

The tunnel was circling downwards through the black

rock. Narrow and low in parts, I could pass through easily, as I thought could Rosa. As for Dad, he would have had to bend his head for most of the way.

Even as I thought that, I wondered how tall the thieves had been? Had they hit their heads on the roof of the tunnel. Had they been able to squeeze through the narrow bits?

At the same time, the tang of the sea was growing ever stronger. Soon I caught the distant sound of water lapping and the breaking of waves. Did that come from outside the tunnel, or inside?

My sense of direction told me we were heading towards the rear of castle rock, and nowhere near the Sea Gate that Granny Beaton and Rosa had talked about.

How had the thieves known about this tunnel if the Chief of the Clan MacLeod did not? Granny Beaton, who knew most of the tales of the island, hadn't known about the secret tunnel either.

So, how had the robbers learned of the passage which had allowed them to steal the precious Fairy Flag?

Despite the power of my nose, I found no scents other than those of the two humans and the dog Fang, so it seemed that no one apart from the thieves knew about the tunnel.

The sound of lapping was becoming louder, echoing

around the walls of the passageway. Wherever I was, it was very close to water.

Even as I thought this, a small wave broke over my front paws.

I stopped, not because I was afraid. I like paddling and swimming. Love it in fact. The question was, would I have to swim to get out of the tunnel?

I waded forward. I have good eyesight as well as a good nose, but the tunnel was so inky black that I couldn't even make out shadows anymore. I would have to rely on my nose alone.

Moments later, as the water reached my haunches, I knew the truth.

The rest of the tunnel was under water because the tide was coming in and swiftly.

Leaving me trapped between the Fairy Flag room and the sea!

Retreating from the water, I sat down to think.

I'm a good swimmer and not just on the surface of the water. I'll go down a fair bit if there's something I want to fetch up. So I could go under the water to get out of the passageway.

The first question was how long could I stay under?

The second, how long is the passageway?

Sitting in the darkness, I could still scent the two

people who had been there, and the dog called Fang. If Fang had been in here with the robbers then he hadn't been afraid and could more than likely swim.

So if Fang could get out of here, then so could I.

My decision made, I stepped once more into the water and began to walk down the slope a little at a time. The water level definitely hadn't got any higher. I know about the tides. We dogs can tell things like that without checking what humans call tide tables.

The tide had turned in the passage and was now in retreat.

Should I wait for low tide and hope the passage would empty completely?

I immediately decided not to. Rosa would be worried about me, and Dad would too. Plus I needed to discover where the thieves had got into the secret passage.

The water level now at my neck, I set off to swim into the darkness.

Something you should know about dogs. Our main sense is smell, followed by sound, followed by sight. That means humans see things better than us in daylight, but we're much better at seeing in dim light.

At first this didn't matter because it was as black as my coat in the tunnel. My nose and ears being happily above the surface, I could hear the blowout from my breathing and the splash of water against the passage walls.

All of which helped my swim through the tunnel until…

The roof suddenly dipped and I had to dive!

Not in the fun way I do to bring back a ball, but just to avoid hitting my head on the roof. I didn't panic of course, but I did wish that I'd taken a bigger breath before it happened.

Dad had timed me diving once and told everyone I could stay underwater for 90 seconds, whatever that means. I don't know about measuring time, I just know how long I've got, before I need another breath.

And I didn't have long, so, just to check the situation above water, I came back to the surface … and found the water level had dropped, thank goodness, and there was room to breathe.

Not much but enough.

Not only that, it was no longer pitch blank. A human might not have been able to make things out, but I could, which meant we were getting closer to the outside and daylight. Plus I could hear something that sounded like waves crashing against rocks.

As I suddenly felt myself being sucked under again, I quickly took another deep breath and then I was underwater and being dragged back into darkness.

Chapter Eight

The Other Side

It was over in moments.

The retreating wave dragged me through what looked like a big hole in the rock, and threw me out on the other side. With a kick of my back legs and a few paddles of my front paws, I broke the surface again… and found myself no longer in the dark.

A little way away, I could see daylight, although in here all was still shadow. I paddled to the sand, dragged myself out of the water and gave my coat a good shake. I had survived the black tunnel and the underwater swim and I was free.

I had a good bark to celebrate.

As I did so, I thought I heard an answering bark. Or maybe it was just the echo of my own voice in the cave. I put my nose to work and immediately picked up the scent of the two thieves again, plus Fang, but I couldn't imagine Fang answering me if he was anywhere about. Not unless he was telling his owner where I was.

That thought stopped me doing any more barking. After all, I didn't want to be caught and held captive. I might be able to deal with a dog, even a dog with a scary name like Fang, but if there were two humans involved in the fight as well, I wasn't likely to win.

I made for the daylight now, which did involve a little more swimming but not in the dark and definitely not underwater… and then I was outside and giving myself another shake!

Once that was done I took a look around. I could see the castle in the distance and was surprised at how far I had come from the Fairy Tower. Rosa, I knew would be frantic with worry. Granny might even have got in touch with Dad about the fact that I was missing.

So the sooner I got back the better.

I was a fast runner and would have no difficulty getting back to the castle and quickly. As I prepared to take off, I suddenly heard the bark again.

And this time, it definitely wasn't an echo of my bark.

In fact it sounded sad, or frightened. More a distress call rather than a warning, or a 'Here I am' kind of bark. I immediately stopped running and stood listening.

There it was again, and to my mind it was definitely a cry for help.

One that I would have to answer!

I gave a loud bark which said in human terms, 'Where are you?'

A moment's silence followed this and I wondered if

the mystery dog was changing his mind about wanting to be found.

To reassure him, I barked again, this time saying something more like, 'Do you need help?'

That too was followed by silence, then by the most terrible sound I'd heard in a long time. The unmistakable howl of a dog in pain.

Wherever the dog was, he definitely needed my help.

I set about sniffing the air, then the ground, running back and forth in the silence that had followed that terrible sound, and eventually I found the scent I was searching for.

I stood stock still, my hair standing out on end, the way it had done just before I'd jumped into the secret passageway.

Something was wrong here and it wasn't my nose!

The scent I was picking up which led into the wood that lined the shore was the scent of Fang, the thieves' dog.

I couldn't believe it. The dog whose cry for help I'd heard couldn't possibly be Fang, so maybe Fang was the attacker? That thought made me very angry indeed. Not content with stealing the Fairy Flag, Fang was attacking a dog in the castle grounds.

I knew all the Chief's dogs. They were pals of mine.

The thought that one of them might be hurt drove me on.

The trees grew closer together as I left the shoreline of the loch behind. I darted my way through, sure I was following Fang's trail, all the time hoping that it would lead me to his poor victim.

As the scent grew stronger, I halted, knowing that the dog I'd smelt from the name tag and whose scent I had followed in the secret passageway was definitely close by.

And sure enough, as I peered through a thicket of whin bushes, I saw him.

Big and black, he matched his name. Except for one puzzling thing. He didn't look fierce. Not one little bit. He was lying unmoving, attached by a rope to the nearest tree. Even stranger, from this distance, I knew by his scent that he was one the one who was hurt.

The question was how badly?

He turned his head as I entered the clearing and made an attempt at a growl, showing his fear and his teeth. I could see at that point why he was called Fang, but neither the show of teeth or the half-hearted growl worried me, because I knew it was because he was hurt and afraid.

A swift look told me that his coat was in a poor condition, and I could see cuts that had bled and then crusted over. It was obvious that Fang didn't have a human Dad like ours to look after him. In fact worse than that, someone had hurt this dog.

I felt anger bubble up my throat and I growled.

Fang met my eye and attempted to stand up, but it definitely wasn't easy, especially when he tried to put pressure on his right front paw.

I asked him if his owners were coming back for him. Fang didn't like that idea at all, glancing round anxiously as though it might be about to happen.

I sniffed at his injured paw. 'Did they do this to you?'

He didn't answer the question, just whined at me to help him get free.

I began immediately, thinking all the time that Laoch would have been very useful right now, my wee brother having chewed his way through much thicker and tougher things than the rope that was keeping Fang prisoner.

To keep his spirits up as I got to work, I gave Fang a list of all the things my wee brother Laoch had chewed.

'All the seats in Dad's truck, one after another. When he'd finished with the seats, Laoch started on the carpet! Needless to say Dad wasn't pleased about that.'

'Then came the handles on the chest of drawers that lives in the woodshed. Dad said removing them was like solving a Chinese puzzle, but Laoch managed to do just that and poof they were gone.'

Fang was almost smiling despite his obvious pain.

'But the thing he chewed most was his own tail! Can you imagine?'

I gave Fang a big doggy grin at that, and I swear he gave me a small smile in return.

'But since I don't have the master chewer here, it's all up to me.'

I went on working at the rope and just as I was almost through the last few threads, I heard the sound of loud voices arguing and feet crunching the twigs in the woods.

By Fang's expression, it was clear he recognised those voices.

His abusers were coming back!

Chapter Nine

A Friend in Need

'Please, you have to go,' Fang whined at me. 'You can't let them catch you too.'

He was right, but I was almost through the rope which meant we could go together, and I told him so.

'I can't run,' he protested. 'They'll just catch us both.'

It was a dilemma. That's for sure. But I wasn't going to leave Fang to the people who had done this to him, so I kept on chewing.

As the noise of their approach got closer, I broke the final thread.

'Come on,' I urged Fang. 'We can make it to the trees.'

I wasn't sure we could, but I wasn't going to abandon my new friend, whatever happened.

The sound of the rapidly approaching voices seemed to spur him on, or maybe he was just worried about me getting caught too.

We'd just made it into the bushes as a tall man with dark hair and a blonde woman strode into the clearing. At first they were too busy talking to notice that Fang was gone, but once they did, it was clear they weren't happy about it.

As they began shouting his name, I felt Fang tremble beside me. I wasn't sure which of the two humans he was more afraid of. The man or the woman.

When they turned as though to leave again, Fang let out a whimper of relief. Not a wise move.

Immediately the woman turned back and began searching for the source of that sound. We both stood stock still but it was no good.

'Over there,' she screamed, pointing in our direction.

'Run!' Fang told me. 'They'll get you too!'

But I had no intention of deserting my new friend.

I stepped out of the bushes. It they wanted Fang they were going to have to get past my fangs first!

I bared my teeth and gave a growl fit for a lion, or so I hoped.

At this the woman halted.

She started to say things in a soft voice. Things I recognised. Roughly translated I'd say it sounded like. 'Here, doggy doggy! Nice doggy, doggy!'

I must say I had no intention of being nice, so I went on growling through bared teeth.

Behind her the man had picked up a thick branch and was coming towards me with it.

I had a choice. I could use what PC Munro had taught me, jump at the woman and bring her down, but then the man would still be free to hit me, or worse, hit poor Fang with that stick.

As I made up my mind to spring, that's when I heard it. The wonderful sound of Rosa's high whistle telling me she was close by.

Close enough to read my thoughts?

I quickly concentrated on the image of the two robbers, willing Rosa to see it and come more swiftly.

Suddenly there was a shout of 'Blaze. Here to me!'

Granny Beaton was here too! Hurrah!

I began to bark and the combination of my raucous barking and the clomp of Granny Beaton's big motorcycle boots coming galumphing through the bushes stopped the robbers in their tracks.

'We're coming Blaze,' Granny shouted. 'We're coming to get you.'

That was enough for the robbers.

The man and the woman took one look at one another, then turned and quickly crossing the clearing headed back the way they'd come.

Seconds later, Rosa burst through the trees and gave me the biggest hug I've ever had from anyone other than Dad. Granny arrived shortly after and I could tell by the size of her smile, she was just as pleased to see me as I was to see her.

Rosa, finally letting me go, turned to Fang who stood shivering with fear or maybe relief that his tormentors had gone. Rosa knelt down beside him and hugged him gently before she gave him the eye, which suggested she was trying to find out what had happened to him.

When she'd finished, she rubbed Fang's ears and whispered 'You're safe now.'

It was at this moment I saw that the other member of the rescue team was Rory. I made a point of showing him how pleased I was to see him, as Rosa had a quick word with Granny Beaton.

'Okay,' said Granny. 'We need to get Fang to the boat. His paw needs fixing and as Rosa says, he has a lot to tell us about the Fairy Flag.'

It took a while to bring Fang to the shore, and then onto the boat, but we eventually managed it.

As Rory tried to start the engine, I could see Fang checking the coastline, worried that the two robbers would suddenly appear from the woods and come charging towards us, demanding their dog back.

I was worried about that too, although I didn't say so. Just kept my nose in the air and my eyes on the trees so I could bark a warning if they did appear.

Eventually the engine roared into life and thankfully we began to move away from the shore.

I stood at the bow with Rosa, enjoying the spray. I even allowed myself a little thought that despite my incarceration in the tunnel we were definitely on our way to solving this mystery, especially now we had Fang, who undoubtedly had a story to tell.

Maybe he even knew where the stolen Fairy Flag of the MacLeods was at this very moment.

As we approached the castle boathouse, I could see our welcoming committee of Rory's Uncle Calum, Dad and Laoch. I gave a bark to tell them how pleased I was to see them.

As we got closer, Laoch began running up and down the jetty, going wild with his usual excitement. Of course without Rosa around to explain, Laoch would have no idea what had happened on our adventure.

What he would know was how worried Dad had been.

I barked again to tell him we were okay, and my daft wee brother, his excitement getting the better of him, launched himself into the water.

Oh no, not again, I thought, expecting him to sink like a stone and have to be rescued.

I was wrong. Up bobbed his head, and away went his paws, and he was swimming towards us, just to show us he could.

Everyone cheered and I barked in delight.

Then it became obvious that although he could jump in and swim about, my daft wee brother had no idea how to get back onto the jetty.

Cue, Dad reaching in to pull him out by the scruff of the neck, making everyone laugh.

One thing about Laoch…nothing embarrasses my wee brother. Deposited ashore, he gave himself a good shake, and went on prancing about in delight.

Now it was time to get Fang, who was a big heavy dog off the boat. There was a little bit of discussion about this among the adults, then Calum stepped in and Granny Beaton stepped out, before Calum placed Fang in Dad's waiting arms.

We all trooped along behind him to the truck, where Fang was laid in the back on the rug used for Laoch and I.

Meanwhile Laoch, obviously looking for an explanation for this new doggie arrival, rushed up to Rosa to try and find out what had been happening.

I heard Rosa give her high whistle and Laoch immediately sat down. Whatever she told him seemed to do the trick, because after that he went in the back of the truck with me and we lay on either side of Fang, to show our support.

While arrangements were being made between the adults, Rosa went over to Rory who stood near the open door of the boathouse.

From my experience Rory doesn't say much and today was no exception. Dad says he talks when it's necessary, but then Rosa already knew that.

Whatever she said to him, he nodded, and after a quick word with Calum, Rory headed over to the truck with Rosa.

So it looked as though he was coming back with us. Hurrah!

Then Granny headed off to tell the Clan Chief what had happened on my big adventure, as much as she knew of course, before collecting her motorbike.

As for Dad, he made a phone call before we drove off. I knew it was serious by the sound of his voice.

We dogs were very quiet on the return journey, even Laoch, although Rosa and Dad had a long conversation, which Rory listened to. As she told the tale, I could see the images in Rosa's head, but of course there were none after the panel had trapped me in the passage. That was something I still had to tell her about.

Even thinking about what had happened in the tunnel made me shiver a little. It's easy to pretend to be brave. It's not so easy to *be* brave. The way I remembered it, I was more scared than brave, and felt very lucky to have emerged from the tunnel and the cave unhurt.

Unlike poor Fang.

I nosed my new friend to show I was thinking of him in his pain and he gave a little whimper in return.

It's not easy to spend so much time on the hills without getting an occasional injury and Dad had always patched Laoch and I up, except when he needed some professional advice, and that's when he would call the vet.

Looking at Fang, I hoped that had been the call Dad had made earlier.

At this moment Dad was listening intently to Rosa's tale of Fang's escape, shaking his head at times in amazement, checking Fang in the rear view mirror whenever the dog's name was mentioned.

After what seemed a long time, because Dad was driving slowly and carefully so that Fang wouldn't be jostled in the back, we came down the hill towards Taigh na Collie.

As we turned into the car park, I spotted a blue truck I immediately recognised.

Good old Dad.

I barked to show I'd spotted the person I most wanted to be waiting for us.

It was the vet and she had come to take care of Fang.

Chapter Ten

A Plan

Dad had lit the fire and the delicious smell of something tasty filled the air. Granny B having roared in on her motorcycle was busy stirring the pot while Rosa and Rory were throwing me a tennis ball, often and far.

I think there was a little bit of a competition going on between them as to who could throw the furthest, which I was enjoying very much.

Laoch had taken off into the woods after a mythical rabbit and Fang, all bandaged up, and fed and watered, lay on a rug inside Taigh na Collie. The vet had pronounced that no bones were broken but there was a bad gash on his paw and some nasty cuts on his head too.

Whatever medicine she'd given Fang seemed to have sent him happily to sleep, which was good according to Dad.

Rosa, Rory and I had yet to have our talk. I suspected she planned to do that after everyone had eaten and things had quietened down.

Rory might not say much, but he knew lots, especially about the hills. If we were planning to find someone, no one knew the island better that Rory, or so Dad says. He was good on the water too. He had a canoe he explored the lochs with. I've been out with him, but not Laoch, because he couldn't swim.

Until now of course!

I suddenly had a picture of the four of us, Blaze Dog Detective and his two intrepid assistants, with Rory paddling us off on an adventure. It was then I spied Rosa's concentrated expression and realised it was probably her thoughts I was picking up, which suggested she did have a plan.

A shout from Dad announced tea time. After my adventure underground I was definitely ready for food, so I stashed my tennis ball and headed for the big table near the fire where Dad was dishing out baked potatoes and stew, and filling our food bowls.

At this moment, Laoch, who hadn't been seen since he'd taken off while Fiona was tending to Fang, suddenly came crashing out of the woods. How my wee brother always knew the exact moment when food was being served, I have no idea.

Now that's a mystery I've never managed to solve!

After tea, Rosa headed down to the burn, myself in tow. Now was to be my chance to tell her all that had happened to me. It was still gloriously light. This is my favourite time of year where the sun barely sets before it lights up the sky again.

The gurgle of the burn, the rustling of the birch leaves and the occasional hoot of an owl seemed the only sounds to greet us on our walk, yet I could hear a multitude of other noises from the woodland creatures going about their nocturnal lives.

I suspected Rosa could hear them too. She always seemed as attuned to the sounds of nature as I was.

When we reached the spot where she had viewed the crystal ball, Rosa stopped and sat down, beckoning me to join her. Then she fixed me with 'the eye' and I began to relive my time in the tunnel after the panel had snapped shut behind me.

Suddenly I was walking down the passageway again, picking up the scents. Then I was padding into the water, retreating, then deciding to carry on even as the tide flooded the tunnel.

I didn't like being under the water. I didn't like being afraid that I might not be able to resurface. Then I was sucked through the hole and flung out into the cave.

I'm out of the cave now and hearing Fang's call from the woods. When I enter the clearing and see him lying there, obviously hurt, I remember a film I watched with Dad where a lion cub finds his dead father. Dad had to turn it off because I got so upset.

Fang isn't dead, I know that immediately, but he's hurt.

I start gnawing through the rope and then we hear the robbers approach and Fang gets even more frightened. I'm as afraid as him but I keep on chewing. Then Fang's free and limping towards the trees.

The next bit is the worst as I realise just how close we came to being caught before I hear Rosa's whistle.

After my playback, Rosa sat for a while deep in thought. When I tried to look at what she was thinking there was only a blank wall.

I lay down beside her, my head on her feet. She was thinking hard but was unwilling to share those thoughts with me. I could only wait until she did.

By the time we walked back I knew what Fang had told her. The robbers had had an old map giving them the location of the cave. From there they'd used Fang to find the underwater entrance to the secret passageway.

They had made Fang swim through. Beating him when he tried to retreat. When he'd barked on reaching the other side, they'd waited until the tide went out before following themselves.

As to getting into the castle, that had been Fang too.

He'd told Rosa that it was just luck. Sniffing round the door, his nose had touched something and the panel had swung open. Worried it might shut behind them, the robbers had wedged it open with a rock.

So those bad people have our Fairy Flag, I thought sadly.

At that thought, an owl hooted loudly and rose above the trees, the width of its wings masking the silvery moon that was helping light our way.

'You're right, Blaze,' Rosa said, her hand on my head. 'But we're going to get it back.'

When we reached the camp, we discovered a decision had been made regarding Fang's future. One that I was pleased about. He was to become Matt's dog and be renamed Buster, because he'd been busted out of prison by me, Blaze Dog Detective!

That meant Buster would spend his days at Ace Target Sports next door to Taigh na Collie.

I could see that Rosa was happy about that. Fang, now Buster, was likely to hold the key to the mystery of where the Fairy Flag was. Once he felt better he might remember more.

Rosa and I had already agreed to investigate what she'd read in Buster's thoughts, but not mention them yet to PC Munro. It would be difficult to explain to a policeman why we should look where we thought Buster was suggesting.

Who would believe that Rosa 'talked dog' except perhaps for Granny B?

It was better if we checked it out first. And that's where Rory came in. Didn't I say he knew Skye even better than Dad? If Rory couldn't identify the possible location in Buster's memories, then no one could.

While the adults doused the fire and tidied up after our feast, Rosa took Rory aside and brought him up to date with our plans. I'm not sure how much she told him about how she knew what she did, but I saw him glance over at me a few times and nod during her explanation.

As Granny B's motorbike roared off into the night, I felt a shiver of fear return. It was up to us now. The police couldn't get evidence from poor Buster, only we could do that.

And I had seen what the thieves were like. They may have left when they heard Granny coming, but if she and Rosa hadn't arrived when they did, Buster and I might not be alive now to tell our tale.

Chapter Eleven

Our Next Move

The next morning we all met at the police station to give a statement to PC Munro.

Of course I couldn't actually give a statement and neither could Laoch. What we could do was indicate in our own way that what Rosa said was true. She was very thorough. I knew that from her thoughts.

She made me a bit of a hero, but she didn't forget Laoch either and his attempts to rescue Fang's name tag, despite the fact he didn't at that point know how to swim.

She didn't try to explain what had happened to me in the tunnel but she did suggest that since the tunnel was under water at high tide and Fang had been injured from his time in there, it was likely I had been very brave to have made my way out.

At this point Dad had patted my head proudly.

Granny Beaton confirmed the story of the three of them rescuing myself and Fang (now Buster) from the two robbers. She described what the robbers looked like and I could see from Rosa's thoughts that she agreed.

All through this, Rory had remained mostly silent, with an occasional nod and an 'Aye' to confirm to PC Munro that what Granny Beaton had said was true. After the humans had all signed their statements, PC Munro produced a treat each for Laoch and I, although I felt it was undeserved.

Okay, we'd worked out how the Fairy Flag had been stolen and we'd rescued poor Buster, but we hadn't found the Fairy Flag or captured the robbers...yet.

PC Munro thanked us then told Dad that our role in the investigation was over and that we should leave it to the police now to find the flag and apprehend the criminals. Our descriptions of the robbers were being widely circulated, and the police were checking cars leaving Skye via the road bridge and the car ferry from Sleat.

'We'll catch them, thanks to you.'

Rosa looked down at me and I knew it was a reminder that our plan would go ahead regardless of PC Munro's words.

After all nothing stops Blaze Detective and his team (I hope)!

'Okay guys,' Dad was saying. 'What are your plans for the day?'

'We're going to Rory's place and he's taking us out in his canoe,' Rosa told him. 'If that's okay with you?'

'Now that Laoch has proved he can swim,' Dad said with a smile. 'That's fine by me. Do you need a lift?'

'Granny said she would drop us off after she does her shopping.'

Dad wished us goodbye and with a warning to Laoch (not me of course) to behave himself and to do what Rosa told him, said he would see us back at Taigh na Collie.

I have to say I gave a sigh of relief as Dad headed off. I had thought our plan to go to Rory's might have gone awry. I think Granny Beaton probably had something to do with its success. She can be very persuasive. Plus she understood that we would go on trying to solve the mystery despite what PC Munro had said.

We set off along the road, our first port of call being to meet with my pal Jax in the Post Office. Jax is a black Labrador who's almost as famous as myself on Skye. This is because Jax is employed as the official stamp licker. On request Jax will lick your postage stamp for you before you put it on your letter. Tourists (and locals) love that.

Living in the Post Office, Jax is a mine of information regarding the inhabitants of Portree and current visitors to the island. Anyway, word had got through to me that Jax wanted to speak to us about our search for the Fairy Flag.

On entering the little Post office which was across the road from Inga Bonk's famous sweetie shop, we found Jax on duty as usual behind his counter, with a queue of three people, tourists by the look of them, waiting to have their stamps licked.

Each customer of course also wanted a selfie taken with Jax and there was much smiling and laughter. Once his final customer was served, his dad told him to take us into the garden.

Once there having shut the back door, Jax and Rosa began their conversation. I was listening in of course and adding anything I thought needed an explanation. Jax has the deepest dog voice I've ever heard and he also has a strong Skye accent and sometimes he drops into Gaelic, the original language of the island.

Rosa doesn't speak any Gaelic, so I had to translate some bits for her.

Laoch, not one to sit around while folk jabbered, had already wandered off to explore Jax's back garden. As for Rory, he had taken a seat at the picnic table and was watching Rosa, Jax and I intently, obviously desperate to know what was being said.

Eventually Rosa told him.

'I gave Jax a description of the two robbers. He hasn't seen them in the shop or in Portree but he'll make sure Jessie the collie who goes out with the post van tells all the dogs on the island to look out for them.'

'What about what Buster said?' Rory asked.

Poor Buster, with his sore head and paw, hadn't made

much sense when asked where the Fairy Flag was now. All Rosa could see was a bay with black basalt stones and sand, a mist and maybe a boat.

When she'd relayed this to Jax, his response had been that Skye was an island with countless bays just like the one Buster had described.

'Our only hope is that one of Jessie's team spots the robbers in their part of the island. Then you'll have to persuade PC Munro to head that way.'

Granny Beaton arrived at this point and seeing our serious faces asked if everything was alright. Rosa told her that Jax and his friends round the postal route would be given descriptions of the robbers so that they could look out for them.

'Excellent idea. Any help the police can get,' Granny B said. 'So are you ready to head for Rory's place?'

I barked a Yes.

'Rory, you'll come behind me on the bike. Rosa, you'll take Blaze and Laoch with you in the sidecar.'

At this point in the proceedings we realised that my wee brother was nowhere to be seen. Since Jax's back garden was surrounded by a high wooden fence, we couldn't imagine how Laoch had got out. While I barked a message for him to come back, the others called his name.

64

Moments later a return bark told us he was on his way, quickly followed by himself leaping back over the fence and landing with a light thump on the grass beside me. My wee brother is like a mountain goat, which can be useful on Skye.

'Just spreading the word,' he told us with a grin.

And, no doubt begging at every back door, I thought, judging by the crumb evidence round his muzzle.

'Let's go then,' Granny Beaton said.

Barking goodbye to Jax we headed out to the motorbike which Granny had left parked outside the Co-op.

'Can you manage to squeeze in with the shopping,' she said, as Rosa set about installing herself and the two of us in the sidecar.

It was a squeeze, but we managed. I warned Laoch not to sniff at the food bag then sat quietly as Rosa put on our new doggy goggles before her own.

Laoch seemed even more excited than usual and I soon learned why. A high whistle from Rosa had got him to sit still enough to learn what he'd been desperate to tell us since he'd jumped the fence back into Jax's garden.

'I know where they are. I know where the robbers are.'

Chapter Twelve

Black Sands and a Red Canoe

We had asked Granny to drop us at Orbost House. By then we'd been rattled about enough on the rough track that wound down the hillside towards the sea, bouncing through ruts and over stones so that my teeth kept knocking together.

Jumping out of the sidecar, I was delighted to have my four paws back on firm ground again.

Before she left, Granny made arrangements when to come back to collect us and then she was off and roaring back up the track towards the road.

As we set about walking into the bay where Rory's home was, I knew he was giving Rosa an explanation as to why he spent so much time during the holidays with Matt at the sports centre or his Uncle Calum at the castle boathouse.

'My mum died when I was wee and my dad's a fisherman, so he's away at sea a lot.'

For a brief moment I saw Rosa's own parents in her thoughts and knew she understood how Rory felt to be alone in the world.

As we turned a sharp corner in the cliff path we saw in

front of us the whole curve of the bay of black sand.

'That's where I stay,' Rory told Rosa, pointing at a white boathouse close to the shore. Above the big double doors were some attic windows. 'My room's up there.'

I could see the pictures in Rosa's mind as she imagined what the attic room might look like with its view of the waters of the sea loch.

Laoch as always, had rushed ahead, keen to prove that his theory was correct. The bay definitely fitted the description that Buster had given Rosa with its black rocks and sand. No mist at the moment, but that was because of the sunshine and the light breeze that ruffled my coat.

But it had been the extra piece of information that had convinced Laoch that he was correct.

Two doors along from the Post Office he'd got into a conversation with wee Hamish, a white Scottie dog whose owner was none other than the wife of a fisherman whose boat was moored in Portree harbour.

According to wee Hamish, he had seen a man and a woman fitting our description of the robbers at the harbour the day before the burglary.

'There was a black dog with them. Poor soul it was. I tried to be friendly to him but they shooed me away. They were asking how to get to the Tables.'

Now to folk not familiar with Skye, that doesn't make any sense, but Laoch knew where they were talking about. Him, me and Dad had climbed both big flat topped hills also known as MacLeod's Tables, which lay directly west from where we were now.

It seemed my assistant was learning fast how to be a detective.

If our robbers had been planning to reach the Tables by sea, this location would have been as good a point as any.

With Laoch bounding ahead, we reached the bay. Rory led the way to the boathouse and opening the double doors, pulled out the canoe. I was familiar with this mode of transport of course. Rosa was not, but she loved the red canoe from the first moment she saw it. I could see it in her face and hear it in the excitement of her thoughts.

'It's beautiful,' she said. And it was.

Hand built by Rory, sleek and red, it skimmed through the water, and with no noise, unlike the motor boat they'd borrowed from Rory's uncle Calum to rescue Buster and me.

Rory slid it down the slipway and into the water, then holding it steady, told us all to get in. My only worry was that Laoch, who wasn't good at sitting still, might rock the boat and tip us all in.

Rosa had already thought of that. After a whistle from

her, Laoch sat as still as a stone, apart from his head of course as he watched for what would happen next.

Thankfully too, the water was so flat and calm, I could see clearly what lay below the surface.

Our plan was to paddle along the shoreline, first west then east. This was a lonely part of Skye and definitely not on the tourist route, but the cliffs and caves along the coast could offer a good hiding place.

If the robbers wanted to escape the island by sea, this bit of the coastline would suit them very well.

As we skimmed across the water, I kept an eagle eye open for any signs of human activity on shore. Laoch was watching too. I thought I'd never seen him stay so still and silent before. My assistant was definitely showing signs of improvement on the behaviour front.

In the distance I could see the big pinnacles of rock called MacLeod's Maidens, jutting out of the water. We were definitely in MacLeod territory around here. If losing the Fairy Flag was important to everyone on Skye, it was most important here where even the mountains and sea stacks carried the name.

The wind no longer rippled my coat. Instead the mist which had appeared atop the two hills was creeping towards the shore and our canoe. A shiver ran through me as it had in the Fairy Tower and I knew something was

69

about to happen.

I looked to Rosa, trying to read her thoughts, but they just reflected what she and I were both looking at. Towering cliffs, the waves breaking at their feet.

We had walked those cliffs with Dad and I knew how easy it would be to lose your footing and fall. From the water the cliffs looked even more frightening, like walls of shining black rock that suddenly appeared, then just as quickly disappeared back into the thickening mist.

Rory paddled steadily onwards, but it was getting harder and harder to see where we were going.

'Stop!' Rosa suddenly said.

Rory back-paddled the canoe bringing it to a halt, while the mist swirled around us like a white curtain.

My hair stood out again from my body and catching a glimpse of Laoch, I saw his ears prick up.

Rosa gave her silent whistle urging Laoch and I to stay quiet and I could now see why. The mist was parting before us, creating a long tunnel on the surface of the water… at the end of which sat a boat.

Black as the cliffs and much, much bigger than Calum's motorboat, it rose layer upon layer above us. As we watched, it turned a little on its anchor and we saw its name painted in red.

The Darkness.

Every hair on my body bristled and I longed to growl my anger because something told me that everything about that black boat was bad. Beside me, I knew Rosa felt the same.

Did this boat have anything to do with the theft of the Fairy Flag?

Chapter Thirteen

Something Surprising Happens

Rory turned the canoe silently in the water. We were heading back the way we had come.

I had moved to sit close to Rosa. Her hand was on my head and it seemed that her thoughts flowed into my own. Buster in his muddled state had spoken of the flag being hidden near the black beach after it was stolen.

What if it was hidden on shore here soon after they'd taken it from the tower? The plan being to collect it later, perhaps when their transport arrived and that transport was the sleek and shiny black boat?

A boat that powerful could go far away and quickly. While PC Munro and the rest of Skye and Lochaber Police were checking folk crossing the Skye road bridge and looking out for the robbers on the island, the flag could be taken from the island by sea.

As we drew closer to the bay, the mist suddenly departed, blown away by a soft breeze. One thing was sure, the mist had provided the cover needed for us to discover the boat hidden along the coast near the Tables and not to be seen by those on the big motor yacht.

Rory beached the canoe. I was out first splashing

through the shallows, then Laoch. As for Rosa, she still seemed in a dreamlike state and Rory had to say her name three times before she realised we were back where we'd started.

After Rory pulled the canoe clear of the water, he and Rosa began heading for the boathouse. I bounded ahead and up the steps. Laoch, apparently released from his quiet mode by Rosa, took off, making for the field behind the beach, no doubt to check out the local rabbit population.

I also wanted to do some investigations myself although not for rabbits, but I wanted to run my plan past Rosa first.

Once inside, Rosa went straight to the large map of Skye that filled one wall of the room. It wasn't like the maps Dad used for our walks together. It look much older than that and had all the old Skye names on it.

Rory came over then and pointed at the bay where we'd seen the black yacht. Then she and Rory began to talk about what we should do now. They could of course tell Dad or Granny Beaton about the boat. Maybe even persuade PC Munro to board it and question whoever was out there.

But what could they tell PC Munro to persuade him to do that? They couldn't tell him about wee Hamish hearing

73

the man and woman at the harbour asking how they might get to the Tables.

Neither could they say that they had come to the black beach because of that story and found a black yacht which they were suspicious about.

Granny Beaton might believe such a tale, but I agreed with Rosa when she said that she didn't see Dad or PC Munro accepting our reasons for suspicion.

So what next?

I came in then with one of my 'listen to me' barks. Rosa immediately came over and gave me the eye. I was pretty sure what I should be doing now and I told her. If Laoch was good at seeing things with his blue and brown eyes, I was the champion sniffer and I knew what the two robbers smelt like.

If they had come down here surely I would catch a scent of them on shore? I had caught nothing on our walk into the bay, but that could mean they had come by car.

We had taken a short cut to the boathouse and we hadn't gone near the parking place behind the beach. So that's where I would start.

Rosa understood immediately and urging me to investigate, said she and Rory would wait here until it was time to meet Granny Beaton.

Glad to be on the move again, I ran down the staircase

to the beach and began to make my way slowly and carefully towards the flat grassed area behind. A beach is a wonderful place for smells with multiple scents of the little scurrying creatures that Laoch always chases.

He's had his nose nipped more than once when annoying a crab. I love the beach, but with the strong smell of rotting seaweed, and the salty scent of the sea, picking up a human presence there can be tricky.

Having tracked back and forward a few times, I now left the black rocks and sand behind and moved up onto the grass. There was a boat parked on its trailer which looked as though it hadn't moved for a long time, plus at least two other vehicles. That's where I focussed.

Here I could pick up the rabbits Laoch was no doubt off chasing, the smell of diesel too, even the scent of Rory who would be here often, but not either of the two scents I sought.

Were we mistaken that the robbers had come here? Were we wrong about the black yacht? In that moment I thought that we would never find the flag, let alone rescue it and put it back in his rightful place.

Just then a rabbit popped up in my sights. It was a big male, plump and handsome. By the size of its feet it could outrun Laoch no bother. Me too probably. It met me eye to eye much like Rosa did.

At that moment we were joined by a crow flying low and cawing above us. My first thought was that it was after the rabbit, yet the rabbit seemed unafraid. The circling crow swooped down towards me instead, then up again, moving towards the east, as though encouraging me to follow.

At this, the big rabbit disappeared as swiftly as it had appeared. Down a rabbit hole I presumed. The crow on the other hand, with a mixture of cawing and swooping, continued to urge me to follow him.

Chapter Fourteen

A Question of Crows

The crow appeared to be heading in the direction of the track we had all walked down earlier. As it neared the cliff face close by the boathouse, a black swarm rose to join it, circling round and round, the sound of their caws filling the air.

Where had all the crows come from? I stood mesmerised by the noisy black cloud above me. At that moment, Laoch came bounding up, his eyes bright with excitement.

'They've come to help. They know about the Fairy Flag. They know, they know.'

'How?' I asked him. 'How do they know?'

'The castle has crows of course. They'll have told them.'

Could this be true? Could the crows be trying to help us in our search for the Fairy Flag? My heart, which had dipped so low earlier, rose again with the sound of their flapping wings and cries.

The constant cawing had brought Rosa and Rory out of the boathouse to stand on the wooden platform at the top of steps and gaze up at the swirling sky.

I read in Rosa's expression that she thought this to be a good omen. She whistled to us and Laoch and I immediately bounded towards her.

The circling crows grew quiet as a single crow messenger flew down to perch on the handrail next to Rosa.

I watched as the crow and Rosa locked eyes, and I knew by Rosa's expression that something was happening.

Seconds later we heard the roar of Granny Beaton's motorcycle as she approached the sharp corner on the access track and came into view.

At her sudden appearance the big black crow rose with a final squawk to join the black cloud and they all flew off, making for the hills behind.

Rosa didn't look too concerned by their departure so I assumed whatever news the crow had brought, it wasn't altogether bad.

Ten minutes later, Granny Beaton was listening carefully to what had happened from the moment she'd left us in the bay. When Rosa explained about the mist and the black boat, Granny Beaton didn't look at all surprised.

'Skye's always been known as the Misty Isle. The mist hides, but it also reveals things, like today. Just like with the crystal ball. Now tell me what passed between you and the crow messenger.'

'They know about the Fairy Flag and they will help us find it,' Rosa told her.

'The birds you saw will tell others,' Granny said, looking very pleased.

So my wee brother Laoch was right. I felt quite proud of him at that moment.

We headed back after that, Laoch and I in the sidecar with Rosa, and Rory riding pillion again. As we passed alongside the cliff face beside the boathouse I remembered the black swarm above it like a thundercloud.

With all this help, surely we could rescue the Fairy Flag before it left the Misty Isle forever?

Arriving home we found Dad had already lit a fire for our cookout. Even better than that, Buster was up and about and looking much better.

He wasn't able yet to rush to welcome us, but the mad wagging of his tail said it all. That and the big grin. Gone was the fearful Fang. He was definitely Buster now. After greeting Buster, Laoch took off into the woods as usual, although after my strange meeting with the large rabbit, I couldn't imagine myself chasing any of his family again.

Well not for a while, anyway.

Dad of course asked Rosa about our day. We had already agreed we would tell him about the black yacht, but not about the cloud of crows.

'What's a big expensive yacht doing anchored down there?' Dad wondered. 'Did you see the name?'

'The Darkness,' Rosa told him.

'Think I'll mention that to PC Munro,' Dad said.

I saw Granny Beaton nod over to Rosa and knew her nod meant we'd succeeded in planting a suspicion about the yacht without any mention of helpful carrion crows.

Success!

After we were all 'fed and watered' as Dad calls it, Granny Beaton, Rosa and I set off to our clearing to check out her crystal ball. I could see despite what had happened up to now, that Rory wasn't at all sure about looking into a crystal ball.

Being a practical lad who had a strong connection with nature and the animals and birds of the island, he might accept their part in the adventure, but a crystal ball was something else entirely.

And so, it was only Rosa and I who were present when Granny's unveiled her crystal ball on top of the tree trunk. In the deep silence that followed, I felt the ripple that caused my hair to stand up on end.

The ball clouded over, swiftly filling the glass with a

white mist like the one that had hidden our canoe earlier. I sat very still, my whiskers standing out like antennae as the mist began to part forming a long tunnel, just as it had done for us, leading to *The Darkness*.

At first its form was hazy as though we were viewing it in bright sunlight, then as it became clearer we realised the yacht was in fact moving, the water breaking against its black bow, its flag fluttering in the breeze.

There had been no flag visible when we saw the yacht, but now there was one in all its glory.

And it looked like the Fairy Flag!

Chapter Fifteen

A Tricksy Warning

Despite Granny Beaton's reminder that the crystal ball was tricksy, I could not erase the image of the Fairy Flag, so old and precious, being taken away by the black yacht.

If that had already happened, or even if it still might, was too terrible to think about.

'We must tell PC Munro something that will make the police board that yacht,' Granny said as the image faded.

But what, I thought?

'The thieves have to escape from the island and if they don't go by car, a fast yacht like that might just be the way.'

'I don't believe the flag is on *The Darkness*,' Rosa said, shaking herself out of her horror. 'But I think it may soon be.'

A shiver went down my spine at Rosa's words.

'If the yacht had come into Loch Dunvegan loads of people would have spotted it,' she said. 'Where it's anchored it's well hidden. I think the robbers hid the flag on shore near there, and waited for the yacht to arrive.'

I suddenly had an idea. I barked to tell Rosa and she immediately fixed me with her eye. As she read my thoughts, I could sense her excitement.

'Blaze says we should ask Buster again. He's feeling much better. Maybe he'll remember something more now.'

'An excellent idea,' Granny Beaton said, 'and possibly more reliable than my tricksy crystal ball.'

She swiftly covered the ball and slipped it back in her bag. I could swear it wasn't happy about that. We headed back to camp, where Laoch was still out on his night prowl and Dad, Rory and Matt were sitting by the fire.

Granny told Rosa and I to go to Buster and have our conversation. Buster would want to hear today's story.

Buster had officially moved next door to Matt's place. We found him lying on the new bed Matt had made up for him. As we entered, he sat up and wagged his tail. He was looking a lot better, and definitely no longer in pain.

Rosa made a big fuss of him, rubbing his ears and whispering words of affection.

I wondered how often that had happened in his former life, and decided probably never. We settled down beside him and I knew Rosa was relating the story since we'd last spoken.

Buster was wide-eyed, giving little whines, and at the point where Rosa told him about the black beach and the squawking crows circling overhead, he suddenly barked.

'What is it?' Rosa said.

They took me to a beach like that before they stole the Fairy Flag, he told her.

We hadn't thought to ask Buster about the time before they'd broken into the castle. Now we learned that he'd arrived on Skye in the back of a van. He remembered a long journey from the city without any windows to look out of.

During the journey the woman had talked on the loudspeaker with another man who had a strange voice, and who seemed to be giving her orders about what they were expected to do.

'They talked about the map he'd given them. And how much money they would get when they brought him the flag.'

I wanted to know why the man's voice was strange and Buster explained he had an accent.

I thought of all the visitors who came to Skye from around the world. Might the man have come from another country?

It seemed that Buster had only been allowed out of the van a couple of times during the journey and on one occasion the van had been parked near a black sand beach.

'Is there anything else you remember about that

beach?' Rosa asked, knowing there were other similar beaches on Skye.

'It was night time. I was only allowed out of the car for a short time,' Buster told her.

'Try, Buster, please,' Rosa urged him.

Buster concentrated, the dressing on his head crumpled in thought. 'There was a building. I remember now. It was white with big doors that faced the sea and a set of steps that climbed to the top'.

My heart beat like a drum as I saw what he was remembering. It was Rory's boathouse.

After that Buster had been shut up again in the van.

'I jumped into the front seat and saw them walk off with a torch and a wooden box. They went up the hill behind the white building.'

Rosa looked at me, her eyes shining and I thought the same thing as her, and at the same time.

They were looking for somewhere to hide the Fairy Flag.

Buster's head had drooped and he was looking tired again. At this point Matt appeared.

'Time for your medicine, Buster,' he said.

Buster wagged his tail at Matt's kind voice and we knew he was in good hands.

'Buster will see you tomorrow, guys,' Matt said. 'He

needs his sleep now.'

We walked back to the fire in silence. I knew what Rosa was thinking because I was thinking the same. If the robbers had been exploring the cliffs to the east of the bay, and carrying a box. Could they have been set on hiding the flag they'd stolen?

When we got a chance to speak to Rory, he thought the same.

'The coastline there is peppered by caves. It could be that's where they're hiding, or maybe they stashed the Fairy Flag somewhere along there to await the arrival of the yacht.'

But the yacht's there already, I thought. Maybe we are too late.

'If the flag had reached the yacht, it would already have left,' Rosa said, reading my thoughts.

'We'll go back tomorrow,' Rory was saying. 'We'll take the canoe along the east side of the bay. If there's anything there, we'll find it.'

After Granny left with Rosa, and Rory with Matt, Dad, Laoch and I sat by the embers of the fire. On nights like this, Dad would sometimes talk to me. I wasn't always certain what it was that troubled him, but tonight I did know.

He wasn't happy about the black yacht, and pulling out

his mobile, decided he wanted to speak to PC Munro about it, tonight, rather than tomorrow.

I wished then that Rosa had still been here, so that I was sure what was said, but after Dad rang off, he patted my head and I knew that he was pleased at whatever had been agreed.

Despite the phone call to PC Munro, I found I couldn't sleep. Every time I closed my eyes I saw the image in the crystal ball of the black yacht sailing away, the Fairy Flag flying from its mast.

Chapter Sixteen

The Approaching Storm

As soon as Uncle Matt arrived with Rory next morning, we set off for Portree. On the way, I tried to listen in as Dad talked to Rory about his conversation with PC Munro the previous night, but without Rosa's thoughts to guide me, I wasn't certain of what was being said.

When we reached the Police Station, we found Rosa waiting for us.

'Granny thinks we should be the ones to explain about the yacht,' she told Dad.

Dad ushered us all inside the police station. PC Munro was there to greet us, and immediately took us upstairs to the big room they use for their crime investigations. I decided that meant that what we said would be taken seriously.

I tuned in as Rosa described our trip along the coast in the canoe, missing out the role of the the mist, to the moment we'd spotted the black yacht. At this point, PC Munro got Rory to show him on a map exactly where the yacht had been anchored.

PC Munro and Dad talked then, and I concentrated on Rosa to try and work out what was being said. It seems that *The Darkness* belonged to a Mr Marcus Loxely, an American businessman and art collector who was visiting Skye on holiday.

'He's been sailing around Skye this past week, anchoring at places of interest,' PC Munro told Dad. 'According to our investigations, there is nothing to suspect him of being anything other than a tourist. I'm sorry,' he added, looking at Rosa. 'I know you want to find the Fairy Flag, but I don't think Mr Loxely had anything to do with its theft.'

Dad asked then about the actual thieves and whether, with our descriptions, the police had had any luck spotting them.

'We've followed a few leads and we may have the registration of the van they arrived in but...'

'You think they've already left the island?' Dad said at this point. 'Or changed vehicles?'

'Possibly. We've alerted our forces on the mainland too, in case they did manage to leave,' PC Munro told him.

We four knew Buster had been brought here from a city, but how could we explain that to PC Munro? Luckily Dad helped us out on that, without realising it.

'They wouldn't head for Inverness. They'll make for Glasgow. I think they must already have a buyer for a private collection.'

'We've alerted Glasgow and Edinburgh airports,' PC Munro told him. 'In case they try to fly the flag out.'

Rosa had remained silent while Dad and PC Munro had been talking. Now she said firmly, 'The flag is still on the island.'

Both Dad and PC Munro turned to look at her.

'How do you know that, Rosa?' Dad asked.

I could immediately see the storm of crows in her thoughts, but if she said we thought they were helping us, Dad and PC Munro would tell us we were just imagining things.

Rosa knew that too, so she shook her head. 'I can't explain.'

Dad patted her shoulder. 'The police will keep on looking here too,' he told her. 'We won't give up.'

No, we definitely won't, I thought, and tucked my nose into Rosa's hand to give her my support.

Granny Beaton was waiting outside for us and by the look on our faces, she could tell things hadn't gone well.

'Okay,' she said. 'I've packed a picnic so you can spend all day in the bay.' She didn't say looking for the flag, but we knew that's what she meant.

Dad looked a little worried as we set off. I suppose he was as upset about the recent developments as we were, but didn't know what else he could do.

It's up to us now, Rosa silently told me.

It was good to be back in the sidecar with the breeze blowing my coat. Plus, I believed Rosa when she said the flag hadn't left the island. Granny Beaton said those feelings were because Rosa had the second sight. She had a sense of where the flag was. Just not the exact place.

As Granny B deposited us at the bay, she wished us good luck.

'I'll be back around five. There's a storm coming in later according to the forecast. It's better if we get you all home before it breaks.'

As Granny's motorbike roared off up the track and silence descended, Laoch, after a quick conversation with Rosa, was given permission to take off as before. His hope being to make contact again with the crows in the woods behind the bay.

Given my wee brother's reputation for chasing anything furry, I suspected if the very large rabbit wanted to meet us again, it would more likely appear to me.

While Rory set about bringing out his canoe and getting her ready to sail eastwards this time, Rosa chose a big rock to sit on and gaze out to sea. There was nothing I could do to help Rory, so I joined Rosa to share her thoughts.

The loch was flat calm, the sky a bright blue with a few small fluffy clouds passing by. Granny Beaton had said a storm was coming. Looking at the sky and the sea it was hard to believe, but raising my nose to the sea breeze, I knew that she was right.

With Rosa's hand on my head, I saw that she was replaying our last visit here in her thoughts, as if she believed there was something she had missed. Something important.

I did the same, hoping that I might spot it even if she did not. After all, we dogs have a different way of looking at the world than humans, even someone like Rosa.

Rory's shout that he was ready broke our dreamlike trance. Rosa rose and with a high-pitched whistle to Laoch to warn him we were ready to go, we went to join Rory at the slipway.

Rory held the canoe steady and Rosa and I got in and made for the bow, my nose already on high alert. As Rory sat down ready with his paddle, Laoch came bounding along the beach in his usual late fashion and had to be dragged aboard by the scruff of the neck.

By his quick exchange with Rosa, I guessed he'd had no luck contacting the crows. In fact, it appeared the woods had been strangely quiet with no birdsong at all.

As we moved away from the boathouse, it occurred to

me that Laoch was right and it was really quiet. In fact the splash of the paddle as it broke the water was the only sound I could hear.

Why was it so silent?

Where was the cry of the seabirds? The lowing of the Highland cattle in the field behind the bay? The baaing of the sheep on the hill behind the track? It was like being back in the blanket of the mist that had smothered all sounds on our previous journey to the black yacht.

Yet there was no mist.

Rory stopped paddling as the silence seemed to deepen. The menacing power of it made my hair stand up again.

Just then a thick black cloud appeared on the horizon moving swiftly towards us, like the storm that Granny Beaton had warned us about.

No ordinary cloud, however threatening, could move as swiftly as that.

This wasn't a rain cloud, heralding the coming of the promised storm.

What was swooping towards us was a storm of crows.

Chapter Seventeen

Cliffs and Caves

The storm of crows was almost above us now and they had begun to form a pattern. They weren't cawing, so the only sound to break the silence was the steady beat of their wings.

We were all staring skywards, the faces of Rosa and Rory a mixture of excitement and alarm, which was exactly how I felt myself.

As the crows moved into position, I realised what pattern they were making. Rosa too had seen it and she called out, 'It's the Fairy Flag.'

And she was right. It was the Fairy Flag, not torn and fragile, but more like the one in the painting we had seen in the tower room.

As we watched, spellbound, a small group of crows broke away and flew towards the shoreline, a little ahead of where we were. They formed an arrow shape, whose tip seemed to be pointing towards a spot on the cliffs close to the headland.

'There are lots of caves there,' Rory said. 'Are the crows trying to tell us the flag is hidden in one of them?'

The storm of crows began to break up with the same

speed as it had formed, the birds flying off in different directions. The three that had made the arrow swept up and over the cliffs heading it seemed for the hills behind.

In that moment the bay and surrounding land came to life again for I could hear everything now. The sound of seabirds calling, the slurp of the sea on the side of the canoe, the breaking of the waves against the stony shore.

Rousing himself from the strangeness of the last few minutes, Rory, his eyes fastened on that spot on the shoreline, began to paddle swiftly towards it. As we sped through the water, my keen ears pricked up.

Was that the chug of a boat engine?

Laoch had caught the sound too and we both barked in tandem, causing both Rosa and Rory to turn, and there it was, the bow of *The Darkness*, edging its way out of the cove that had been its harbour.

We all held our breaths for a moment, unsure in which direction it would turn. PC Munro had said Mr Loxely was anchoring all round the island. Could the yacht be heading further west?

I wished really hard that it might.

The seconds that followed seemed to last forever before the bow of the black yacht turned and began to sail in our direction.

As soon as Rosa realised that the yacht was coming our

way, she thought of the storm of crows and the arrow pointing to the spot ahead of us.

Had those on the yacht seen that too?

That terrible thought was swiftly followed by another, as Rosa imagined the canoe being hit by the wash from the big yacht, and us all being tossed into the water.

It was like the forewarning Rosa had had of Laoch drowning and it worried me as much as Rosa. We could all swim, even Laoch now, but where would we swim to?

There wasn't a shoreline at this bit of the coast, just the black cliff, stacks and hidden caves. And how far could Laoch swim anyway?

Looking upwards, I could see nothing that suggested we would be able to climb up the towering cliff face, even a sure-footed collie like myself.

As the waves from the advancing yacht began to rock the canoe, Rory started paddling, making for what looked like a cave opening.

Glancing back, I saw we were hidden by an outcrop of rock, but not for much longer. Even as I thought this the sharp bow of *The Darkness* swept into view.

'Quick,' Rosa shouted to Rory. 'Before they see us!'

Rory's rapid strokes brought us swiftly into the shelter of a natural arch in the rock. We all sat very still, holding our breath, listening to the big engine as it passed us by.

Eventually Rory said, 'After this arch there are a row of caves along the headland. I think the arrow was pointing in the direction of the last one. It's the deepest and there's a beach at the far end we can land on.'

'You think that's where they've hidden the flag?' Rosa asked.

'I don't know, but it's the only cave that has access to the headland above.'

Rory began to paddle through the long arch towards daylight on the other side.

Rosa and I were still in the bow so we emerged first. At first there was no sight of the yacht and we assumed it had gone on further. We were wrong. The engine sound had stopped because the yacht wasn't moving anymore.

Rory, hearing Rosa's warning and my accompanying growl, immediately brought the canoe to a halt.

'What is it?'

'The yacht's dropped anchor,' Rosa told him. 'I think it's close to where we're going.'

Rory eased forward a little so that he might see too.

'It'll be difficult to get past them without being spotted,' he said. 'We'll have to keep close to the cliff face.'

'What if they're here to collect the Fairy Flag?' Rosa said, her voice breaking. 'And we can't stop them?'

Feeling her distress, I nuzzled her hand.

Silence fell as we all contemplated what might happen next. I was remembering the terrible vision in the crystal ball. Even as I thought it, Rosa told Rory what she'd seen there. How the black yacht had flown the Fairy Flag as it sailed away from Skye forever.

'You said the crystal ball plays tricks sometimes. What you saw there isn't what has to happen,' Rory said.

'But sometimes it's right,' Rosa said. 'Like when it showed us how to get into the secret passageway.'

At that moment, a big black crow came swooping down to perch on the bow of the canoe. Its dark beady eyes stared unblinkingly at us, before it rose and flew a little ahead.

It wants us to follow, I told Rosa.

Chapter Eighteen

Hide and Seek

As we emerged the sun had disappeared behind thick grey cloud. Our crow guide was a little in front of the canoe, flying from perch to perch along the cliff face.

With the sun gone, our path through the water was covered in shadow. I was sure the crow was intent on keeping us hidden from anyone who might be looking through the windows of the black yacht.

It wasn't long before we reached what looked like the first of the caves. Nearing high tide, the entrance was just visible above the surging water. I wondered if, when we reached the right cave, we would be able to get in at all.

'Are you sure we'll be able to get into the cave with the beach?' Rosa said, voicing my concerns.

'Yes. It has a much higher roof,' Rory told her.

All the time we had been moving slowly forward, we had been drawing nearer to the stern of *The Darkness*. Now we were the closest we had ever been and the big yacht seemed to tower above us, its name written in blood red along the stern.

I could also see a smaller motorboat on the lower back deck, ready to launch. If that happened I wanted to know and quickly.

My nose was busy scenting, and I was sure that if either of the two robbers should emerge on deck I would smell them. Laoch had been using his keen eyes to scan the landward side of our route and his radar ears were listening for every sound.

As we reached the entrance to the second cave, the crow gave a warning caw. Rory reacted immediately, paddling the canoe into the shelter of its entrance. Laoch gave a low growl beside me as he spotted the bulky figure of a man appear beside the motorboat.

My nose picked up a human scent, but it definitely wasn't one of the robbers. I told Rosa so.

We waited in the shadowy entrance until eventually the crow told us all was well again.

Outside, the sky had grown darker and I could scent the storm Granny B had warned us about.

Rosa, picking up on this said, 'The storm will be here soon.'

Rory nodded. 'If we can make it to the third cave we can pull the canoe up on shore and shelter from the storm.'

We set off again, keeping as close to the cliff as possible, the crow guiding our way. With the appearance of each dark shadow in the rock, I hoped it would be the cave we were heading for.

'Almost there,' Rory finally said to Rosa, as though reading our minds, 'but we have to pass the yacht to reach it.'

The wind had risen and with it the swell. The water of the loch had grown as dark as the sky, and the rocking shadow of the black yacht loomed over us only a short distance away.

I could just make out the dark wings of the crow in the dwindling light as it flew directly at what looked like the cliff face itself.

Rory tried to follow, his paddle scraping the rock we were so close.

At that moment, the big yacht turned again and now there were two men on the back deck, looking our way, or so it seemed.

Would they spot the red canoe? If so, what would they do?

Moments later, we were picked up by an incoming wave and swept inside the final cave and silence fell.

Rory handed Rosa a head torch like Dad used on our night walks.

'Don't switch it on until I tell you,' he said. 'We don't want them to see the light.'

As we moved further inside, I began to make out more

and realised that daylight was filtering in from above. As we turned a sharp corner we heard the sound of waves breaking on a pebble beach.

'Okay,' Rory said, 'you can turn the torch on now.'

The beam from both head torches showed up everyone's startled faces. Laoch's eyes looked even stranger than usual and I knew my shaggy coat was standing on end.

'Let's get ashore,' Rory said.

As he dragged the canoe up onto the stones, I jumped out and began to have a good sniff about. If the robbers had been in here, surely I would be able to detect them?

Above us a glimmer of grey confirmed what Rory had told us. There was a way into the cave from the headland above.

I checked now for our crow guide but there was no sign of him.

'I think the crow's job is done,' Rosa said, patting my head. 'It's up to Blaze Dog Detective now.'

And his team, I thought.

As we began our search for the flag, we could hear the storm outside growing wilder. The waves that had swept us into the cave had grown in size and were now crashing against the pebble beach. We were okay in here, but the black yacht would be getting hit pretty hard outside.

Where they were anchored now wasn't as sheltered as before. The force of the sea against the headland was what had caused all the caves to form in the first place.

Rosa was thinking the same and hoping that the yacht would head back to where it had been anchored earlier.

If it did, that would give us more time to check the cave for the Fairy Flag.

I'd covered the shore by now and found no scent of the two robbers. The beach according to Rory was sometimes washed over during storms or at really high tides, so maybe any scent of their presence had been washed away.

Or...

They hadn't been in the cave at all.

Rory had seemed certain that the crows had pointed towards the cave, but I was beginning to wonder if that was true. What if they'd been pointing at the headland?

I went over to Rosa and gave her my thoughts.

As we all looked up at the faint circle of light, a big drop of water hit my nose.

If it was raining outside, some of it was finding its way in through the shadowy crevice above.

It was time, I decided, for me to explore the upper entrance to the cave.

Chapter Nineteen

Buried Treasure

'Be careful,' Rosa shouted after me as I began my climb.

The route I chose was steep and slippery in parts, but manageable to a sure-footed dog like myself.

Dad never worries about me when we're climbing mountains or when we're walking the cliffs. Laoch is another matter. He has to be kept on a lead at the dangerous bits. So I definitely didn't want him following me.

I'd explained this to Rosa, and she'd immediately brought out the food Granny B had packed to keep Laoch occupied while I climbed.

Jumping from ledge to ledge, I eventually got close to the roof where I began to smell rabbit, which suggested there were burrows nearby.

I thought of my rabbit scout, who had forewarned me of the arrival of the crows. Would the rabbits who lived around here have any knowledge of what had happened to the Fairy Flag?

A flash of lightning lit up the opening as I approached, followed swiftly by a roll of thunder. The storm was right above us and it would be wild out there. Squeezing through the opening, I emerged onto a grassy hill dotted with rabbit holes.

The wind had risen since we'd paddled into the cave. The sea was dark and choppy, and bobbing up and down on it was the black yacht.

So the yacht hadn't left for a more sheltered cove. Could that mean this was their arranged meeting place?

I turned away from the sea to find what looked like the big rabbit from earlier sitting up, front paws in the air, staring at me. I looked around in case our crow guide would suddenly appear too, but it didn't.

The rabbit turned and loped further along the hill, glancing back at me as though it wanted me to follow. When it reached a large rock, it stopped and began digging.

It was then I caught scents I recognised. Going closer, they became stronger.

The two robbers had been here at this very stone! Now I knew why the rabbit had brought me here. Now I understood why the crow's arrow had pointed here. The robbers hadn't been in the cave, they had been above it.

No dog can dig faster than me when I have a bone to bury, so I set about digging where the big rabbit had shown me. It wasn't long before my scrabbling paws came across something and it wasn't a buried bone.

When my claws scraped against wood, I stopped and did a bit more sniffing. One of the robbers had definitely handled what looked like a box to me. I was so excited by my find, I gave a loud bark.

My bark seemed to break whatever spell had made me forget the storm, because suddenly I noticed the torrential rain beating down on my head and the wind nearly blowing me off my four paws.

It was then I spotted what looked like the headlights of a vehicle coming along the hill towards me. Were the robbers coming back to collect their hidden treasure?

My joy at finding the box became fear that I was about to lose it again.

I didn't know what was in it, but I thought, or hoped that it would be the Fairy Flag so I couldn't leave it here for the robbers.

I began to dig madly round the box, clearing the soil away from the sides, and then I found what I was looking for… a handle.

If I could grab it with my teeth, I was sure I could pull the box out of the hole and drag it somewhere. But where and would there be time?

The lights of the approaching vehicle were growing bigger all the time and it was definitely heading in my direction. I would have to be quick.

My jaws firmly round the the handle, I began to pull. With the rain beating down, the hole I'd made had already begun to fill with muddy water. If I lost my grip would I be able to find the handle again?

As I tugged even harder, I wondered what I would do with the box if I did manage to get it out. Could I drag it across the wet and slippery grass and find another hiding place before I was spotted?

It was at that moment that Rosa came into my thoughts.

Of course I had a place to put it, I realised. Safer than any other and completely out of sight of the approaching robbers, but I had to be quick.

With one more big tug, the box was free and on the grass.

As I began to pull it towards the hole in the cave roof, I heard the vehicle come to a halt only yards away. With a quick look back I saw two people get out, a man and a woman. I knew immediately it was the robbers and they'd come for the box.

The headlights were still on and I could hear their raised voices over the noise of the wind. Then one of them gave a shout. They'd seen me!

My jaws are strong, but holding the metal handle and pulling the box over rough ground was making my teeth ache. Just at that moment the box hit a big stone and I lost my grip of the handle.

As I struggled to get a hold again, I saw a torch beam bouncing towards me.

They were only yards away when I got a hold again. I was close to the hole in the cave roof but maybe not close enough.

They were shouting at me now. Stupid words like, 'Come here' and 'Good boy' and 'Drop it!'

One of them darted towards me. It was the man and he had a big stick in his hand, which he was waving about as he tried to hit me.

I could have got out of his way, but that would have meant abandoning the box and I wasn't about to do that! Besides I was almost at the hole.

And there it was.

I dropped the handle from my mouth, barked loudly in a warning to those below, then gave the box a shove with my muzzle and it was through and falling.

I heard Rory's startled voice and then I caught Rosa's shout directed at me and what she said was 'Run, Blaze. Run!'

Chapter Twenty

Don't Mess with Blaze!

I heard Rosa's shout, but I didn't run.

Instead, I turned and faced the robbers. I don't often bare my teeth, but I did now. Just like in the woods when I was protecting Buster. In fact I was thinking of poor Buster at this point and what they'd done to him. All those cuts on his head and the horrible wound on his paw.

The man, still brandishing his stick, came to a halt at my warning growl.

He might have got away with beating a poor tied up Buster, but if he tried to hit me, I planned to take a big bite out of his arm.

I think he realised this because he began to back off. The two of them had a conversation, before the woman took out what looked like the radio Dad uses when we go out with the Mountain Rescue Team.

As she talked, a big search beam of light found us on the hilltop. At first I hoped it might be the coastguard helicopter come to look for us, then I realised it was coming from the sea. In fact the piercing yellow beam was coming from the black yacht.

The woman was telling the men on the yacht where the

box had gone, which meant they would send someone into the cave to get it!

I had to warn the others.

I began to edge my way towards the cliff edge and the opening, my teeth still bared in a warning. The man, spotting what I was up to, came running at me again, his face furious, the big stick swinging.

I snarled at him, then turning quickly, leapt down through the crevice into pitch darkness. Unable to see where I was going I landed badly, and had to scrabble to get a firm foothold.

Rosa was the first to realise I was there and the beam of her head torch sought me out.

'Blaze!' she called, her voice a mix of relief and concern.

I picked my way carefully down the steep rock ledges, scenting the safe path that I had chosen on the way up.

Laoch came part of the way to greet me. I had never seen my wee brother so happy. He was almost doing somersaults.

When I finally reached the beach I went straight to Rosa. The box stood open beside her. Inside was a sealed package doubled-wrapped in plastic. I gave it a sniff and knew.

It was the Fairy Flag of the MacLeods!

We have to leave and quickly, I told her. The people on the yacht know the box is here in the cave and they'll be on their way to take it back.

Even as I said this, the big beam of light that had found me on the clifftop swept across the cave entrance and I could already hear the sound of an approaching outboard engine.

'They're coming for the flag. We have to get it away from here,' Rosa told Rory.

But where, I thought? We can't go up the way, and we can't leave the cave the way we'd come in.

Rory was explaining something to Rosa now. Her thoughts were tumbling one over the other and I found them difficult to follow. I saw a tunnel in the rock, much lower than the one we'd come in by. Was there another way out of here?

Rory was pointing to the right of the cave. There was a passage he told Rosa, but there was little headroom at high tide, which was now. We couldn't all hide in there with the canoe.

We couldn't, but *I* could, I told Rosa. I was a good swimmer, I could go under if need be, just like in the secret passageway. I could hide the Fairy Flag, but would it be safe from the water?

Just as Rosa said she thought it would, the searchlight

hit the entrance, and the chug of the engine echoed off the cave walls. We had no more time to decide. Our pursuers were already here.

Lifting the precious package lightly in my jaws, I ran to the far right of the beach. Keeping close to the cave wall, I began to swim, my muzzle clear of the water. The flag had been carefully wrapped up to protect it, but I didn't want to take any chances.

'Just there!' I heard Rosa shout.

I turned right as instructed, and sure enough there was a small opening in the rock face, with enough room to enter.

A little way in, the tunnel roof rose giving me plenty of headroom. Even better I could see a little light in the near distance, which suggested the tunnel by its direction might be another way out of the cave.

It was at that point I heard an extraordinary sound. A sound I knew the meaning of. A tumultuous echo of squawking and flapping of wings was heralding the arrival of a flock of crows inside the main cave.

Whoever was in the dinghy didn't like that one bit!

There were frightened angry shouts, swiftly followed by the definite sounds of a retreat. I would have barked my delight at this, but couldn't for fear I would drop the precious bundle.

As the noise of the crows' attack faded, I re-entered the cave, to find both the crows and the dinghy gone.

Had the birds chased the dinghy all the way back to *The Darkness*? I hoped so.

I headed for the beach, the Fairy Flag still held gently in my mouth, to find no sign of my friends. The canoe was still drawn up on the beach, but neither Rory, Rosa or my wee brother Laoch were anywhere to be seen.

Had the men from the black yacht captured them before the crows arrived?

I quickly swam to the beach and dropping my parcel a safe distance from the water, I gave myself a good shake. After that I sniffed the air. For Rosa. For Rory. For Laoch. For all of them. When the only scent was so faint I thought it must be old, I howled my distress and anger.

I had saved the Fairy Flag from the robbers, but I'd lost my friends. My howl rang round the cave, bouncing off the walls. The sound only made me sadder.

It was then I heard it. The whistle that no human could hear!

Rosa was somewhere in the cave. I looked up and there she was. Soon Rory's head appeared nearby. Last but not least, I heard Laoch's piercing bark as he came leaping down from on high, looking more sure-footed than I remember.

I wanted to hear what had happened while I'd been in the tunnel, but I didn't think there was time. The men from the black yacht would likely come back. They knew the box was in the cave. Plus they probably thought I was there too, but had they come in far enough to spot the canoe, or had the crows stopped them before they'd seen it?

Whatever the answer, we had to leave here and soon, I told Rosa.

Rory listened to my description of the side passage from Rosa. 'We can't leave by the main entrance. If they spot us, they'll be after us, and they can move a lot quicker than we can. If Blaze is right, we might just scrape through the tunnel in the canoe,' Rory said. 'We can definitely try.'

Rory waded into the water, pulling the canoe with us inside, behind him. Taller than Rosa, he began swimming just short of the wall of rock. I was pleased to find the outgoing tide had provided headroom for the canoe and all of us if we lay flat.

I was at the back, my nose and ears on guard for the possible return of the dinghy. As the wall of rock came swiftly towards us, Rosa pressed Laoch as close to her as she could.

Rosa and Rory had switched off their head torches and

114

we were in complete darkness. In the silence that followed, I could hear the brush of Rory's hands on the rock wall and the scrape of the canoe's sides as he manoeuvred us forwards into the narrow tunnel.

Rosa, a hand on Laoch's head was sending out words of comfort. We would come out the other side, she was telling him and head for the boathouse. She even pictured Granny Beaton coming roaring down the road to rescue us.

I liked the pictures Rosa painted, but I still wondered how we might escape without being seen from the black yacht. A canoe, even paddled by Rory, couldn't outrun a powerful outboard engine.

At that moment, my radar ears picked up the swish of a paddle from the main cave. The two men were coming back, this time quietly, the engine turned off.

As Rosa picked up on my thoughts, she whispered them to Rory. The canoe was brought to a halt. Now the only sound was the light slap of water on the tunnel walls.

I suddenly realised there was a chance the robbers wouldn't know that Rosa, Rory and Laoch had ever been in the cave. As far as we knew they hadn't seen us enter and they had only seen me with the box on the cliff top.

They no doubt thought it weird that I had pushed the box into the cave, but to them I was just a dog like poor

Buster.

Having landed, we now heard them crunch over the pebbles, calling to one another. I scented two people, neither of which were the robbers on the cliff top.

By the sounds of their voices they weren't happy, because they could find no trace of the box on the shore. Plus they were puzzled as to where I had gone!

Then there was a shout of joy. One of them had climbed up to the first ledge and found our carefully planted box.

It all depended now on whether they would check inside or not. If they believed no humans had touched it, and the box was firmly shut, why would they?

A dog can't open a catch like that.

Deciding they were making enough noise not to hear any sounds from us, Rory began pulling us slowly through the tunnel again. Eventually the roof began to rise and slowly but surely we emerged in front of the cliff face.

The wind had dropped, although the surface of the loch was still choppy. *The Darkness* was visible, rising and falling on white-crested waves. I could see the empty stern of the black yacht which meant the dinghy was likely still close by.

Just then, I heard its engine start up again and a few

moments later it emerged from behind the rocks and headed for *The Darkness*.

We must go, I told Rosa. Before they realise we're here.

Chapter Twenty One

Let Battle Commence

As we approached the boathouse, with no sign of being followed, Rory and Rosa seemed relieved, but I wasn't sure it was over...yet. I'd last seen the two robbers on the headland. I wanted to know where they were now.

My inner clock also told me that Granny Beaton should be here to pick us up by now. Why wasn't she?

I scanned the track and the parking area close to the black beach, but there was no sign of any vehicle, neither Granny Beaton's motorbike or a stranger's car. Where had the robbers gone after they'd found me with the box?

My concern about the robbers and the whereabouts of Granny B had been picked up by Rosa.

'What do you want us to do?' she said.

I told her to to go straight to the boathouse and stay there. That I planned to check out if the robbers had been in the bay, or were still up on the headland. I then instructed Laoch to be on guard and if the robbers did appear, he should protect Rosa, Rory and of course the Fairy Flag.

Laoch bared his teeth and gave a menacing growl to show he meant business.

I gave him one more order. One I hoped my wee brother wouldn't need to carry out. He sat up straight at that, his eyes glistening and I knew I could trust him.

I jumped out of the canoe as soon as we neared the shore and headed for the road and parking place, my nose looking for any evidence that suggested the robbers might have been there.

When I found none, I then headed up the track intent on making for the headland where I'd last encountered them.

The rain had stopped and the wind had become a breeze. There was also the hint of sunshine breaking through the dark clouds. If that was a good omen, why was I so worried?

Checking for *The Darkness*, I spotted it still at anchor. I was certain that by now Mr Loxely would have discovered the box the men had brought back was empty, which would tell him that I hadn't been alone in the cave.

The two robbers had seen me with Granny Beaton and Rosa when we'd rescued Buster in the woods, so they would think we were a team. Mr Loxely had gone to a lot of trouble to steal the Fairy Flag and no doubt paid the robbers a lot of money for stealing it.

He wouldn't like the idea of being tricked by a dog, a wee girl and an old lady, which made me even more afraid for Granny B.

I'd reached the spot on the headland where I'd faced up to the robbers. Their scent was everywhere, but so was another scent I'd been searching for. Granny Beaton had been here too and recently. She must have come looking for us. If so, where was she now?

She'd dropped us a little further up the track the first time she'd brought us. As I thought about going to check there for her motorbike, I spotted a car approaching that I didn't recognise.

As it passed me, I realised it contained the robbers. The woman was driving and the man was sitting in the back with someone I couldn't see properly.

Might it be one of the men from the black yacht? Might it even be Mr Loxely himself coming for the Fairy Flag?

I began to race after the vehicle. It was then I heard the high-pitched whistle, and I knew it was coming from the car.

The only human who could make that whistle, apart from Rosa, was Granny Beaton. Granny B had been captured and was in the back of the robbers' car!

The car had speeded up, rattling down the track towards the boathouse. I wouldn't be able to catch it up…unless… I took a shortcut.

I left the winding road and headed for the cliff to the east of the bay. If I could make my way down the rock face there safely, I would be at the boathouse before them.

As I took off in that direction, I saw to my horror that the motorboat had left the black yacht and was zooming its way towards the bay.

The baddies were coming from land and sea to take back the Fairy Flag. Plus they had captured Granny B!

I'm a fast runner when I'm running after a tennis ball, but I bettered my best speed I think on this occasion. Reaching the cliff top in double quick time, I carefully picked my way down the steep gully behind the boathouse, my mountain rescue training coming in very useful. While I did this I formulated my plan.

We would have to attack on two fronts. On land to free Granny B. On the beach to prevent the men coming ashore.

Reaching the beach I found that Rory and Rosa had built a big bonfire and were about to light it, hoping to attract the coastguard.

Laoch was there taking his guard duty very seriously. I told him what he had to do next, which made his eyes light up with excitement.

I now headed for the car park as the robbers' car come down the final stretch, with just enough time to hide myself behind the old boat. Surprise was to be my first weapon. The second, my snarl and teeth.

As the car drew up beside the old abandoned boat, I waited, tense and at the ready.

The man got out first, but I didn't go for him. The woman was the one I wanted. She'd always sent the man after me, in the woods and on the headland. Which meant she was likely more afraid of me than he was.

When she stepped out of the front seat, I sprang at her.

She screamed but that didn't stop me from grabbing her arm and wrestling her to the ground.

The man came to her aid, but without a stick what could he do? Nothing.

Granny took her chance, as I knew she would. She was out of the car and heading for the boathouse.

I kept my hold on the screaming woman until I saw Granny B reach the others, then I let go and ran, barking madly, towards the sight of the fire leaping high in the air, visible for miles around.

I spotted Laoch there, waiting for the two men who were about to reach the beach.

My wee brother was daring them to do just that. His ear curdling high pitched bark was in top form. The snarling and snapping jaws defying either of them to put a foot on dry land.

I joined in, knowing we might hold them back for a while, but if the two robbers joined them we were in trouble.

At that moment, a huge dark cloud appeared on the horizon, as black and brooding as the earlier storm, but moving more swiftly.

Rosa cried out in joy, realising what it was.

'The crows are coming! The crows are coming,' she shouted.

The men looked up at the advancing swarm, and I could see fear on their faces.

An engine roar from the car park signalled the departure of the robbers. They too had seen and heard the flapping wings and loud caws of the approaching birds.

But the birds had no intention of letting any of their prey get away.

As the car tried to turn for its escape, a section of the flock landed on it, blinding its occupants, and bringing the car to a screeching halt. Needless to say no one tried to get out.

Another air battalion of crows were landing now on the dinghy and its occupants, covering them in a black blanket. The two men weren't going anywhere either.

The rest settled around us in a protective circle, on the boathouse roof and on the rocks and on the black sandy beach.

It was then I heard the joyful roar of Granny's motorbike and spotted Matt riding it, followed by another vehicle I knew only too well. Dad was coming down the track in our truck, followed by two police cars, one no doubt driven by PC Munro. While from above came the steady beat of the approaching coastguard helicopter.

We were saved, but even more importantly, so was the Fairy Flag.

Chapter Twenty Two

The Fairy Flag Comes Home

I'd been on the coastguard helicopter before, but Laoch hadn't and neither had Rosa or Rory. Their eyes were shining with excitement and happiness.

In the case of Laoch, both colours were!

We were heading across the island towards Dunvegan Castle, the baddies having been arrested. According to PC Munro, *The Darkness* had also been escorted into Portree along with everyone involved in the theft of the Fairy Flag, including the yacht's owner, Mr Marcus Loxely.

We, on the other hand were on our way to return the Fairy Flag to its rightful place in the castle. The evening was clear and bright, the storm that had raged across the island already forgotten.

I watched with interest as we passed over some of the roads we had travelled in search of our precious cargo and soon we were circling over the castle and the woods where I'd found and saved Buster.

Dad and Granny Beaton had set off ahead of us. I suspected Granny B had raced her motorbike to the castle with Dad on her tail.

As soon as the police had arrived the black army of

crows had risen and parting into numerous groups, they'd flown off to their usual hunting grounds.

As we came in to land on a grassy area near the entrance, the castle crows called their welcome from the battlements and this time they sounded happy.

We could see the chief of Clan MacLeod waiting for us, plus Rory's uncle Calum and what looked like the entire castle staff.

If dogs could cry, rather than howl, I would have shed a tear of joy. I could see one in Rosa's eye and many of the other people there, as Rosa handed over the parcel that contained the Fairy Flag. When the Clan Chief accepted it, there was a tear in his eye too.

As people took photographs of the flag's return, the Clan Chief said Rosa, Rory, Laoch and I would have free entry to the castle forever, and we were to come back as honoured guests when the castle had its open day to welcome the Fairy Flag back to its rightful home.

Afterwards, we all chose to go back with Granny Beaton. Rory riding pillion and Rosa, Laoch and I in the sidecar.

All in all it turned out to be a very special day, especially when we arrived back in Portree and found everyone waiting for us outside the police station, including Jax from the Post office, Jessie from the post van and wee Hamish too.

Best of all Inga Bonk was there with more than one tray of her special tablet, and everyone including Laoch and I, were given a piece as a reward.

After all the photographs and all the patting Laoch and I got, we headed home where Dad lit a fire for our barbecue. Laoch as usual rushed off into the woods, while I sat with Rosa sharing our memories of what had happened.

After we'd all eaten our fill, Dad brought out his guitar and the humans had a sing song.

Me, I climbed the hill and sat down to watch the road that leads to the Fairy Glen and Dunvegan Castle. If fairies did exist, I imagined them coming out in the summer twilight to dance with joy at the return of their flag.

As I did so, I noticed a big black crow had come to sit on a tree stump beside me. We looked one another in the eye and I barked a *thank you*.

He squawked, and flew away.

The End

Blaze says …

If you've enjoyed reading *The Magic Flag*, please take time to post a review online if you can. This is always helpful to authors like Dad.

If you are planning a visit to Skye, Laoch, Dad, and I can take you on guided walks to hidden gems on the island. Details on our website: **https://blaze-walks.com**

BL🐾ZE'n'TR🐾ILS

No visit to Skye would be complete without trying out the activities on offer just outside Portree at ACE Target Sports. Watch out for Uncle Matt and Buster! See the ACE website for info: **https://www.ace-skye.com**

For the grown-ups, don't miss reading my Aunt Lin's crime thrillers. I helped her with one of them and was the first Dog Detective to appear at the Edinburgh International Book Festival. Find out more about her and her books at the Lin Anderson website:

http://www.lin-anderson.com